FIRE DRIFTER 2: TRAILS

By Carol Bellhouse

Cover Design by Dawn Beck

Copyright 2013 Carol Bellhouse

Published by Zuni Canyon Institute

Some of this is true.

Most of it isn't.

You decide.

I lay it down at 120, the surging power of the Camaro under my fingers, wheels spitting fire, taking the curves 1-2-3. Mine for the taking. Mine for the asking. Like life.

Carol Dellhorn

1971

Chapter 1

The sky cracks. I hear it as I hear Landry's heartbeat, his breathing. I open my eyes and all the stars are gone from the sky. They have rained down on us and are lying as spent as we are.

The roll of thunder is long and hard. Nothing will ever be the same again.

Landry is still inside me. I feel the burning but am paralyzed. I listen to the fracturing of the heavens. Devoid of stars, the blackness of the night is complete.

I realize I'm shaking only when Landry tucks me underneath him. His mouth rest in my neck and the warmth of him protects me from cold shivers but cannot stave off the quaking in my soul.

I turn my head to the windows and see the lightning as it shimmers on the far side of the mountains. The silhouettes of the peaks are as familiar to me as my own face.

Landry's lips move against my shoulder. I feel his hot breath and hear him say, over and over, "Oh, my God."

I inhabit my body but am outside of it at the same time.

Nothing will ever be the same.

I can't really tell if a massive storm is brewing or if the glass of the Opera House windows is reflecting something back to me--a reflection of what I want this to be. Or what it is.

Landry's mouth finds mine and he kisses me, brushing my lips, the softness of his skin as fine as sunlight. His kisses are slow and dazed. At least he's able to move. My limbs are in disarray, sprawled on the cot where they fell in collapse. I have no control of them.

"Maddie," he whispers.

I open my mouth to respond but there's no air in my lungs. Nothing will ever be the same.

A blast of wind rattles the old windows. The thunder caps claw their way over the Divide and across the sky into Leadville. The rain summits after a long, weary climb and rolls toward me.

I lie under Landry's weight, watching the natural phenomena outside the sinuous glass.

No rain falls. Instead, there are only firestorms of lightning and waves of thunder.

Landry does not seem to notice.

I feel him reach for the bedroll on the floor with one hand. Deftly he jerks the tie and releases it. He pulls it over us. I realize I'm still shaking.

"Maddie," he whispers again.

I feel him moving out of me slowly, trying not to hurt me. He rolls onto his back and pulls me into his arms.

My arm lays lifeless across his chest. I figure sooner or later I will stop feeling like I'm in an iron lung. I want to believe it anyway.

"I've never felt anything like that," he says quietly.

I try to find words but my mind is blank, washed clean of the format of language, of the structure of voice.

Movement returns to my fingertips and I caress his shoulder. His skin is electric, as if it has tiny sparks jumping from the surface. The smoothness of his body is trance-inducing.

"That was amazing," he whispers.

A slash of lightning illuminates the room in the Tabor Opera House where we have hidden away. Landry notices the storm for the first time. I realize he has had his eyes closed.

He watches the jagged streaks of light as they course across the valley toward us. There's a definable front to the storm and it will envelop us shortly. Buffets of wind foretell the power of its impending arrival, pummeling the Opera House and its leaky windows.

"Is this the part about blowing up solar systems?" he asks.

I smile and the smile turns into a soundless laugh. There still is no air in my lungs so I make no noise.

He chuckles because he senses my smile against his shoulder. He feels the laugh in my belly.

I'm reintegrating myself, slowly but surely.

I become aware of the music from the talent show in the theater downstairs. I recognize the opening chords of *Sunshine of Your Love*. If anything is going to blow the power board tonight, it's a band called The Grilled Cheese Incident rocking this song.

Clyde's guitar licks climb through the floorboards. He kicks in with his vocals, "It's getting near dawn."

Clyde is Landry's cousin. Landry should be downstairs, watching his cousin perform, instead of naked with me upstairs where I've made love for the first time. Where we've made love for the first time.

The talent show is almost over. The applause at the end will be loud enough to drown out the storm. There will be a mass exodus. The set will be struck. Everyone will leave. They'll never know we were here. As long as we're quiet.

"I'll be with you when the stars start falling," sings Clyde. I can tell the audience is on its feet. The building vibrates from the music, the foot stomping, the amped-up sound of the guitars, the drumbeat, the whistling and clapping.

It's a glorious night. Even if I'm paralyzed and speechless, it's what I wanted it to be. What I knew it could be. I was able to give myself completely to the experience and I was transported by the power of it.

I was right.

"The light's shining through on you," comes Clyde's voice through the floorboards. He's right too. The lightning display taking place outside the windows is magnificent--electrified, flashy and full of noise. We're incandescent in the storm.

I watch Landry as he watches the furious gale. I know the music is burrowing its way under his skin also. His heart beats in rhythm to the music. His eyelashes are thick and heavy as he blinks. If there were words, we would probably be saying them. He's holding me tight, sheltering me in his arms.

He seems to know. He kisses me slowly. I feel something inside my heart as big as the Rocky Mountains—it's my connection with Landry. But it's mine and it cannot be put to words.

The guitar solo rocks the house.

"You okay?" Landry asks quietly.

I pause for a moment. "Yes," I say softly.

It's okay. I'm okay.

Lightning flames the sky and the roar of thunder melts into the baseline of the guitar.

"I've been waiting so long to be where I'm going," sings Clyde.

The storm is on top of us. It devours Leadville.

Downstairs The Grilled Cheese Incident reaches the crescendo of the song. Clyde bawls out, "In the sunshine of your–."

Then there's nothing.

The music stops. The light in the room goes out. The town goes dead. The darkness and silence are complete. And there it is—it isn't the song that takes out the power board in the Opera House. It's the storm that takes out the town.

Chapter 2

The sudden silence is infinite. The static thunder rolls through the mountain valley. The booming has stopped. Something like a hiss descends.

Downstairs there are cries of surprise and hesitant shuffling in the darkness before the weak emergency lighting system turns on.

"What happened?" asks Landry.

"Storm took the power out," I say but we both know.

Electricity isn't a given here. Conditions are too tough. It's a privilege, not a right. We learn to adjust.

The clouds settle into striations outside the window of the Opera House. It captures the light in layers as the lightning continues. It looks like a black-and-white World War I movie. The lightning no longer resembles nature but a Hollywood construct.

"What will they…" starts Landry.

I answer him with a lingering kiss. "They'll go. They'll find their way out."

"Show's over?" he asks.

"Yeah," I answer.

Sure enough, there's a murmuring from the theater as the audience ponders whether the power will return shortly. They know it won't. They know it will be hours. It always is.

We listen to them groping for their coats, folding up their seats. The band's drummer tentatively strikes a riff. The audience laughs. Someone whistles in the dark.

I whistle quietly in response, the tune from *Meteor Shower*, the monologue with which I started off the talent show ninety minutes ago. It garnered a big ovation from the audience and provoked my flight into the night when I saw Landry at the top of the theater.

I reflect on all that has happened in the last few hours, in the last day, in the last week. I've had a ramped-up, finger-in-the-light-socket life. It's been this way since the beginning. Leadville's drinking and violence are symptoms of the effects of altitude on a populace already too unstable and too adventurous.

As I whistle, I think about the talk that prompted Landry to leave in the middle of the night.

I tried to explain to him why I wanted so much more from sex than what is prescribed for it. I wanted something earth-shattering, something divine, something radiantly powerful.

He fled. In the last twenty-four hours, he has followed the course cut by the Arkansas river to his home in Pueblo and beyond, to the flatlands, to think. Driving and thinking, the cure for everything.

But he came back, appearing in the theater by the door through which I exited at the end of *Meteor Shower*. I stop whistling.

I don't know what there's to say. My body feels radiantly powerful. I'm smug in knowing I was right--that sex is so much more than they would have us believe. Media, society and government must have a big stake in cheapening sexuality.

The voice of Francie Wilbur, my mentor and theater teacher, carries without amplification across the theater. "That's it, folks. Thank you for coming. Sorry about the abrupt ending. Please be careful as you exit."

She has been anxious about this event since I talked her into it. I sold her the idea as a display of talent and possibility of the senior class. The first show of its kind. Probably the last.

She was concerned about the power drain on the old light board. I laughed and chalked it up to an opportunity for one more great story. I hope she sees the humor in the storm shutting it all down.

I, like Landry, should be downstairs. Instead, we're secreted in the upper warrens of a century-old opera house, warm under a dusty bedroll on a convenient cot, illuminated by the shimmering outside. The light warping through the wavy windows makes it a palace like no other. This place does not exist in real time.

"You've stopped shaking," whispers Landry.

I run my fingertips across his chest, his shoulders, his arms. Landry's hands, slow and warm, caress my back and hip. Our nakedness together is beautiful.

"Yes," I whisper back.

The grand staircase groans under the weight of the audience as the theater-goers find their way out of the building under meager emergency lights.

We hear the doors push open and the conversations outside on the sidewalk, discussions of wind and the lightning crossing the sky laterally, caught in the sheeting of the clouds. The thunder rolls horizontally also.

There's no precipitation in the storm. It has simply come across and covered us like a blanket.

"I could touch you forever," I say silently. I don't say it out loud.

Landry's body is sleek and polished. I run my fingers through his hair, the heavy darkness of it. His face is fine-grained and flawless. I touch my finger to his lips and find myself kissing him again, drawn in by magnetic force.

He responds, getting hard and moving toward me. He thinks better of it. I'm sore and burning and he must know it. He stops and settles in to gentle kissing.

Sex is new to me. All the kissing and flirting have not prepared me for the intensity of what I experienced. My body thrums on a wavelength with which I'm not familiar. At least I've stopped shaking. My arms and my legs are my own again, not helplessly scattered across the cot.

"Where will they go?" asks Landry as the audience clears the theater.

Outside car doors slam. Engines start. Music from eight-track tapes and KOMA spills into the night.

"Home. Or the woodsie," I respond. There's no place else to go. With the power outage, the bowling alley will be shutting down. So will the bars. The restaurants cannot prepare food.

I hear a roll of drumming. The percussionist for the Grilled Cheese Incident plays to an empty house.

"Yeah," he shouts. It's rebellious, a standing-up to what is and what we all come to accept in the harshness of this climate. There was one more song to go and they didn't get the chance to play it.

"That's the intro to *Strike Anywhere*," I tell Landry. "Clyde wrote it."

I heard it in rehearsal. Clyde is so proud of it and rightly so. The words flow to the music with an unsubtle, driving beat.

"Great lead-in," responds Landry.

The song may be lost to time now, as the three band members go into the mines. I hope against hope they'll hold the band together and become international superstars. But everything is against them now. They'll be tired after their shifts. The mines will grind them up.

The air smells heavy with ozone from the storm and our sex. I run my fingers across his neck and breathe in his smell—salty, clean and warm handsomeness.

Downstairs the band strikes the set, loading equipment into trucks parked in the alley by the stage doors. There's laughter and complaining but what else can be done?

"What?" asks Landry.

I realize I've said it aloud. "What else can be done?"

I kiss him lightly and stretch my arms over my head. "I hope they remember to shut down the light board."

"Why?" he asks.

"When the power comes back on, it will light this place up." I'm being too responsible and I know it. I wonder if they'll shut off the furnace, the cumbersome, cantankerous old boiler in the basement. It will be cold for us in the night but they do not know we're here. They'll never know we were here.

The last of the footsteps resound on the staircase. I hear Francie and another voice, probably Evelyn Furman who owns the Opera House, as they struggle to lock the front doors. It's always a chore, requiring mild profanity and several pounds of patience.

I lie enveloped in Landry's arms. The night grows quiet with the grumbling thunder playing out and losing its fierceness. We breathe in unison. Silently we watch the lightning run sideways across the sky. It's liquid color, moving from red to gold to silver. It's the color of our earth, the rocky striations of our mountain home. It's rich and brutal.

As the night chill moves through the drafty building, Landry and I bundle closer together into sleep. Landry holds me all night. I dream about a mountain lion. I think I catch a glimpse of the lady in white, one of the ghosts inhabiting the Opera House, but I'm not sure.

Chapter 3

I feel Landry stroking my shoulder. We have been sleeping. He's whispering something, low and easy. I can feel the entire length of his nakedness against my back and legs. We're spooned together. I know it can't be morning.

I remember where we are. The rolling thunder has stopped. There's silence in the air except for our breathing. Landry's voice on the back of my neck creates puffs of hot air against my hair. He runs his hand down my hip and leg.

"Open your eyes, pretty girl," he's saying.

I don't want to. I moan and cuddle deeper into him.

"It's worth it. I promise you," he whispers.

I reach over my shoulder and grasp a handful of his hair. He's really, really here. With me. In the upper reaches of the Opera House. Naked and warm. We're deeply alive.

I open my eyes.

Outside the arched windows the storm has been replaced by a meteor shower.

The stars are back where they should be, blazing in the sky. The meteors are dancing rockets, the heat of their flight making traces across the sky.

It must be close to dawn. There's no way of knowing.

Landry runs his fingers up the back of my head, raking my hair away from my neck. My hair falls across the pillow and my shoulders. I feel its coolness. Being so long, it's always colder than my skin. It slides heavily over my breasts, pooling around my nipples.

His lips on the back of my neck send voltage down my spine. His mouth is warm and wet and sets me on fire.

He kisses me there, flicking his tongue across my hairline. No one has ever kissed me there before. It's a magical triangle, hidden under the weight of my hair. He has found it, knew it was there.

The heat of his breath moistens my flesh. A physical thrill races through me.

"Why is this so easy?" I whisper.

"This is what you were made for," he sighs.

There's gentle strength in his leg as he encompasses my hip with it. Hooking my knee with his foot, he maneuvers me onto my back. He kisses me full on the mouth and I return his fervency.

I wrap my arms around him. My hands clutch the thick darkness of his hair.

"Maddie," he moans.

I stretch my arms over my head, luxuriating in the movement of my muscles. He strokes the softness on the inside surface of my arms, trailing his fingers across the sensitivity of the hollows and curves to my breasts.

"Ooooh," I breathe out.

I want his hands on me like this, in the night, hidden away, under a meteor shower. Everything in me wants this.

His lips find the valley at my collarbone and he bites, tenderly, playfully. His teeth, those perfect white teeth that snapped me to attention the night he smiled at me in Dunn's bar, the night we met, sink lightly into my flesh and tug gently.

I'm sure I'm sliding off the mattress. My body is responding lavishly.

I grab onto the frame of the cot over my head to prevent the movement I'm creating with my arched back and dug-in heels. I'm pushing up into him, taking us both off the small bed.

His teeth let go and I can sense his smile against my collar bone. He runs his hands up the length of my arms, pulling his weight onto me and releasing my grip on the frame. He entwines his fingers with mine, holding me in place, and kisses me, his mouth strong and full.

"Let me have you," he whispers.

The words have come from deep inside his chest. I feel the reverberation of them against my breasts, in my throat, across my belly.

He's claiming me on an animal level. The ferocity of my body's response astounds me.

"Oh, yes," I say, everything in me yearning for him. I wrap my legs around his hips, feeling the leanness of his torso. He hesitates, unsure of the newness of this to me, but I take him. I'm so wet I pull him into me with the pressure of my thighs.

His breath catches. I throw my head back because I need the oxygen. I need to grab for the air that has vanished from my lungs.

"It's like dying," I hear the words and realize I've said them.

I do not hear Landry's response. I'm deafened by the roaring of the force unleashed in me.

Who am I that making love can topple universes, light up the sky in nuclear holocaust, destroy all concept of magnetic wavelength, time and spirit?

Chapter 4

I smell like Landry. He smells like me. And there's the distinct scent of us together, a pungent, sexual aroma I've never smelled before, partly because I'm unfamiliar with this and partly because it's us. And we have not been before.

I'm giggly and giddy. Being with Landry is like dancing in sparkles. The stars that fall when we make love feel like radiant glitter on my skin. I feel buoyant, lighter than air. I'm floating above the bed, weightless and carefree.

I love the adoration in his fingertips, the focus in his kiss.

It makes me feel luxuriously beautiful, being wanted like this. I can't stop smiling. He's repeatedly moaning, "Mmmmm," until it sounds like the pacing of a song. It makes me laugh. Everything makes me laugh. I'm drunk on his love.

I stretch like a cat, basking in every part of my body. I feel alive and adored. I trace his body with my fingertips and I trace mine too. It's all electric. My fingertips tickle from the way our skin feels.

The sun's rays are teasing the mountain peaks to the east, playing in shafts of light across the valley and illuminating the iridescent snow on the peaks.

It's cold.

We made love with only the light from the heavens. I glance up and the light is on. Dawn has restored power to this isolated little community nestled in the valley surrounded by giants.

I kiss him playfully. He laces his fingers in my hair as I rain kisses across his lips.

"Wow, you are really something," he says.

"Am I?" I ask. I've never been more than I am right now--the culmination of all that has come before and the promise of all that is to come to me.

Sunshine floods the valley.

Church bells begin ringing. The Presbyterian Church on Harrison Avenue clangs its melody, followed by the Catholic churches.

Landry and I are lost in each other.

The world outside our windows might as well be light years away. The sounds are so recognizable to me but are now transformed for all time. The world has exploded, the solar system has disintegrated and the stars have fallen to earth. I've experienced something that cannot be described. It's pure and phenomenal. And I know, for sure now, that what the outside world, the world outside this brick building, has done with sexuality is hideous. I love that I was right. I laugh and my stomach growls.

"Hah!" I exclaim.

As if given permission, Landry's stomach growls also.

"A duet," he announces.

We realize we could easily die here in the Opera House if we don't venture in search of food. We have no choice. It's a demand of being human.

"Damned inconvenient," I laugh, our reverie interrupted by reality.

Throwing off the bedroll with dramatic flair, I scamper to the bathroom and start the shower. It will take a few minutes for the hot water to come up from the basement.

I use the time to brush my teeth and relieve my bladder. Between my legs, I'm throbbing and burning but it doesn't hurt anymore. It's a mosaic of sensations that substantiate my admission into another world.

I step outside the bathroom door and beckon Landry. "You. Come here."

He grins indulgently and pads across the floor to me. It's the first time I've seen him naked in daylight.

His skin is so smooth it's glossy. He glides across the floor like a big cat, his legs powerful. The way he moves thrills me to my core.

I give him a few moments of privacy in the bathroom. He swings the door open and pulls me in. "You," he says. "Come here."

I squeeze my eyes shut. I'm so happy

He kisses me vibrantly as we jump into the running water of the shower. It feels heavenly. We soap and shampoo each other, using the sudsy water to explore each other's bodies in the new context. We're wet and warm. And starving. Our stomachs rumble as loudly in the small shower as the rolling thunder from the storm last night.

We're delirious from sex and starvation. Everything makes us laugh. Reluctantly, but knowing our lives are at stake, we turn off the shower and dry each other with the towels I hid under the sink last summer.

As we pull on our clothes, I recount the cartwheel contest at rehearsal yesterday.

"My showing was magnificent," I proclaim.

"Prove it," he insists.

I oblige, launching into a series of spirited cartwheels across the ballroom floor, ending at the windows and bowing elegantly. Landry applauds and holds out his hand.

We must eat or die.

Chapter 5

The J-Mar Cafe is quiet this morning on the heels of the party we missed last night, the graduation woodsie. Everyone is asleep in their cars or sleeping bags or the few who made it home, in beds. The churchgoers are in church.

Landry keeps touching me as if he doesn't want to break the connection between us. I'm fatigued and sore in a way I don't understand. It goes deep into the bones of my pelvis and legs and radiates up my spine into my shoulders and arms.

Margaret, the owner of the cafe, comes over with menus. The J-Mar is our high school hangout, our place to go. I order the steak-and-egg special, medium rare and scrambled. Landry chooses the beef burrito smothered in green chili.

Margaret pats me on the shoulder. "Great job last night," she says.

"Thanks."

Landry smiles at me, his eyes reflecting the light from the windows.

As Margaret walks away, Landry reaches across the table and takes both of my hands in his fingers. We look at each other, searching each other's eyes.

What does one say at breakfast after a night like that? When the heavens showered down? When lightning and thunder slashed open the sky? When we found each other and created something more immense than the mountains and the horizon could encompass?

Margaret brings my orange juice and Landry's coffee.

"Thank you, Margaret," Landry says for both of us.

Landry's coffee steams. My orange juice is tart. It splashes on the back of my tongue in a delicious way. I hadn't realized I was so thirsty. I go for the water glass and down it. Landry is impressed.

"Here's what I think," he says.

I raise an eyebrow as I set the glass down.

"Let's go to Mount Princeton Hot Springs," he says.

I stare at the empty glass. Listening to his words, I can almost feel the warmth of the mineral springs and the heat of the water on my weariness. It sounds heavenly. It will reconnect me with myself and fix the out-of-body sensation I have not been able to shake. The thought of soaking in a hot springs sounds perfect.

I nod, looking up at Landry.

"Let's stay there," he continues.

"What?"

"We'll get a room. Spend our time there, together, until…" He doesn't finish.

I nod. It's the way I need it to be.

The food comes out of the kitchen quickly since we're the only customers. Margaret delivers it with a flourish and the ever-present orange slice.

We eat with relish, listening to James Taylor sing *Fire and Rain*. His voice is mellow and easy. The food hits our empty stomachs and we become giddy. I get the giggles when Landry glances flirtatiously at me through his eyelashes.

Hunger is a given in my life. With the violence and drama at home, there were never meals. On the few occasions when dinner was served, it always ended with someone getting backhanded across the table and knocked into the wall. It wasn't worth the effort.

My brothers and I learned to steer clear of anything that smelled of danger. Mealtime was dangerous. So was sleeping. We took to retiring with baseball bats beside our beds, in case our father decided to kill one of us in the night.

But here and now, I'm eating a delicious breakfast at the J-Mar Cafe on Harrison Avenue with the most beautiful young man I've ever laid eyes on, Landry Lucas.

It's a beautiful, sunny morning, the air scrubbed clean by the weather of the night. A few fluffy clouds scud their way over Mount Massive.

"I've seen sunny days that I thought would never end," sings Taylor. *But I always thought that I'd see you again*, I sing to myself. It's a beautiful piece of music.

"Ready?" asks Landry, picking up the check.

I nod and melt in the warmth of his smile. Maybe, just maybe, starting this moment, the sunny days will go on forever. I can wish.

Leaving the J-Mar, we crash into Clyde, Landry's cousin. He has run through the door. He looks from Landry to me to Margaret and back to me. He's shaking and his face is white. He tries to assess the situation and I can tell the assessment isn't going well. Obviously he didn't know Landry had returned.

He gasps out the words, looking straight at me. "Henry drowned in Twin Lakes."

Chapter 6

We should be used to it by now. It started in eighth grade, when Kenny Morgan was killed in a car that missed a curve and hit a tree, exploding in the night. We die. We die fast and we die angry.

I stand there looking at Clyde's stricken face.

Margaret swings around the counter, her voice anxious, "Henry Dill?"

Clyde nods his head.

"Lord Almighty," intones Margaret. "Have mercy on Tom and Lucinda." She's praying for Henry's parents.

I've had my share of run-ins with Henry. A week ago I knocked him into the bar at Dunn's before I had time to pull back. He had come on to me, aggressive and cold.

It was the night I met Landry.

But despite our differences, he's still one of us. He's a member of the Class of 1971, newly-graduated, a mediocre basketball and baseball player in the shadow of Steve Wadsworth. A living being who no longer lives.

"What happened?" I find the words.

"Someone dared him to swim the Narrows," explains Clyde.

"When?" asks Landry.

"An hour ago, maybe two," says Clyde.

"I heard the sirens go by," says Margaret. Her eyes are turning red.

I didn't hear the sirens. I look to Landry and he glances back. We must have been in the shower.

"Were you there?" I ask Clyde.

"No," he answers. "I went home at about two. They left in a group. Went out to Twin Lakes to party on the beach. Built a bonfire. You know. I guess they woke up this morning, still half drunk, and it happened."

My arms flush with blood, turning hot and numb. Landry reaches for my hand and I wonder if he notices my pulse throbbing in my wrist.

Clyde continues, "Steve called for help from the General Store. And word got around fast. I came looking for you."

He glances from me to Landry. His eyes drop to my hand in Landry's. He begins registering that a lot has changed in the past twelve hours.

"I saw Landry's car," he says and puts it all together with a solid thud.

"Mercy, mercy," wails Margaret. "Not another one."

Chapter 7

Two lakes formed by glacial activity reflect the grandeur of Colorado's tallest peak, Mount Elbert. I'm not looking at the scenic beauty. I'm looking at a confluence of emergency vehicles, lights flashing, and knots of people standing on a cold shoreline.

Landry is twenty minutes behind me, stopping by Clyde's house to say goodbye to the family.

I get out of the Camaro. As I walk toward the gathering, the crowd parts and I move directly into Steve's arms. His cheeks are grubby with tear marks. He is crushed, no longer the effervescent young man who cavorted at Dunn's Bar and danced ballet on the high school bleachers with me.

"Maddie," he breathes tearfully into my hair.

"Steve."

He holds me. I hold him back. We're supporting each other as the conversations resume around us.

A yell comes from the lake, from one of the boats bobbing on the water at the Narrows, the division between the upper lake and the lower lake.

We turn to see a diver holding the side of the boat talking to a deputy. The deputy has yelled to Sheriff Balltrip to get his attention. The Sheriff stands by his patrol car, radio in hand.

We all watch. The deputy leans over the diver to hear him more clearly. He stands upright, meets the eyes of Sheriff Balltrip on shore and shakes his head.

"They haven't found him," I say, the realization as cold as the shoreline wind.

"No," affirms Steve.

"It's Twin Lakes."

Steve nods, knowing. A lot of people die in Twin Lakes. They never float to the surface. They vanish for all time. It's a beautiful, breathtaking place that keeps what it takes.

I look up at Mount Hope and think about how many people have stood on these shores, hoping against hope.

Sheriff Balltrip motions Steve to his car. Steve reluctantly lets go of me and stumbles across the sand to the Sherriff's car.

I look around, identifying the camping group by the disheveled hair and sandy jeans.

The bonfire has been forgotten, laying ashen and smoky in a fire ring. It's a group of twenty and they have sobered up quickly. I go to each of them, holding tightly until I feel some semblance of calm replace the jagged storm crashing inside them.

This is the first time for some of the sophomores. They may have heard of the previous deaths, may have known the younger brothers and sisters. But now it's immediate and devastating. It's "a kid I went to high school with." What lingers is the unspoken reality, "And it could have been me."

I watch Sheriff Balltrip and Steve turn as a car pulls up. Henry's parents have arrived. Tom Dill is so furious and volatile that he has trouble getting out of the car.

He leaves his wife, Henry's mother, in the passenger seat. She remains there, small and mousy, warily watching her husband slam the car door and rush toward Steve and the Sheriff.

Steve backs away as Tom Dill engages Sheriff Balltrip in a heated shouting match with threatening gestures.

The sodden conversations at the shoreline fade into silence as the accusations shouted by Tom drift across the sand and out onto the water.

Two auxiliary deputies maneuver closer. When Tom takes a swing at the Sheriff, they grab the angry man and put him in the back of the patrol vehicle.

I look at the Dill family car. Henry's mother, Lucinda, quietly dabs her nose and eyes with a handkerchief. I start to go over to her when Steve climbs in the driver's seat beside her, closing the door behind him. I see him reach for her hand and I know he will do his best.

Chapter 8

No one is saying who made the dare. We all know it will come out in time but for now the group has closed ranks. That is the one detail not forthcoming.

The story I've pieced together is that the dare began early in the morning, as people were rousting from sleep, still feeling the effects of a night of beer and pot.

Henry was never one to pass on a dare. His bravado and ego were his foundation and ultimately his weakness.

"Swim across. You can do it."

The taunts had finally driven him into the water.

The group began shouting encouragement as he swam. It is only a hundred feet but the cold got him half-way. The shouts of encouragement grew louder and more desperate as they watched him flounder, his lips turning blue. And in an instant he was gone.

No one had gone in after him. It would have been futile. They realized the gravity of it too late. It was over in a heartbeat.

A few express a theory that he's still alive, surfacing on a shore downstream. Without a body, there's always the hope.

When my brother, Joel, disappeared, it produced the same effect. The effect continues still. It hangs in the air, unspoken, unrelenting--the possibility.

It's what gives me the weight and respect of the crowd at this disaster. They all know about Joel. They know I'm Joel's sister. They know I have waited as they are now waiting. My hope has been suspended in the crossfire of reality for five years.

The sun begins to warm the magnificent but heartless lakes. There are murmurs about a professional dive team coming from the Front Range.

There will be no body, I think. Henry will be forever lost in Twin Lakes, another story to be told in late evenings.

My last encounter with Henry had been ugly and brutal. He never liked me and I never liked him. The disdain had escalated over the years.

I had not seen him at graduation but then again I had kept my eyes glued to the stage, purposely avoiding Clyde's questioning glances. I had blown out of the building as soon as it was over.

I'm here for these two frightened juniors who are huddled in my arms when Landry and Clyde approach.

The girls are sniffling, shaking from the abrupt reminder to their young bodies that mortality lays coiled an instant away. It's something our souls refuse to disclose to our bodies. It's a fact best cloaked in the daily tasks of life.

Not saying anything, Clyde and Landry add themselves as an extra layer to our huddle, stretching their arms to enclose all three of us.

We spend the next hour blanketing as much grief and fear as we can. But there's no body. And there never will be.

Chapter 9

We're all exhausted from the cold wind, the strong sun and the senseless waiting. Hunger has driven off most of the original group of campers.

Steve gets out of the Dill car, leaving Henry's mother with her handkerchief, and returns to talk to Sheriff Balltrip. I walk over to join the conversation.

Clyde and Landry sit by the fire, focused on a young man who played basketball with Henry and Steve. He's having a hard time with it and is glad to have someone to talk to, to make an attempt at sorting through the crush of emotions.

"She's holding her own," Steve is saying as I approach.

"Are the girls coming in from Denver?" Sheriff Balltrip asks.

Henry's older sisters work in Denver. Henry is the baby of the family, the only boy.

Steve nods. "They're on their way."

It's going to be bad.

The Sheriff watches Henry's father, Tom, standing like a black force, angry and sullen, at the shoreline. No one has spoken to him since releasing him from the patrol car. He has said nothing to anyone. He's locked in his anger and blame.

Even his wife knows better than to approach him. She sits alone in the car. A senior girl opens the door and climbs in with her.

"Thanks for being here," the Sheriff says to me.

He's aware that my presence has brought a calm sense of experience to the shoreline. I'm a reminder that these situations can take a long time, that there probably will not be a fast conclusion. It just goes on and on and on.

I nod my head in appreciation.

Steve reaches for my hand and I clasp his with both of mine. He's heavy with fatigue.

"It's what happens," I say to him.

His head jerks to the side. I know he doesn't believe it. He probably never will. I don't think the dare originated with him. It isn't his style. But he, like the others, continues to cover. No one is pushing the issue yet.

Everyone knows the name will be disclosed in time. It will be said at some point. And everyone will know and it will be filed away in a collective consciousness.

Life will go on. Life always goes on. Henry will sink into the sediment of the lake as some strange reverse biological process pushes his body down instead of raising it. He will join the others at the bottom of these lakes. And time will continue to pass.

"Why don't you go home and get some rest," suggests the Sheriff.

Steve and I look at each other. He's right. They'll continue searching. It will become more technical as strangers come on the rescue operation. It will be just another rescue scene to them. It will no longer be personal. The investigation will be catalogued in a state archive. The strangers will remark that it's another senseless death so common to Leadville. They'll look down on us. Then they'll close the file.

I walk Steve to his car. There's a long hug and no words. I close his car door as he slides in. He rolls down his window and I kiss him on the cheek.

Chapter 10

The sheets feel divine as Landry pulls them over us. He kisses me sweetly on the forehead.

I was impressed by his cool capability at the beach. I've seen his strength under fire and he's seen mine.

We said goodbye to Clyde at Twin Lakes, receiving his silent blessing. He went home. We drove to Mount Princeton.

Our room overlooks the pool, its white concrete and blue water set off against the white chalk cliffs.

I fall asleep, dreaming in colors—deep blues, crescent oranges, rolling blacks. I'm too hot and then I'm too cold. But I know I'm safe and where I need to be. There was no reason preventing us from coming down to the Hot Springs. I've done what I could.

When I wake an hour later, the numbness has left my limbs. Landry reaches out to touch my face.

"Are you hungry?" he asks.

"Starving."

"There's a restaurant."

"Sounds wonderful," I say.

It's 3:30 in the afternoon when the waitress brings our salads. We pick up our forks, happy in the thought that cheeseburgers and fries will be coming right up.

It's a quiet meal, easy and relaxed. A lot has happened since breakfast at the J-Mar. It feels like weeks have passed. For some of the survivors, it undoubtedly feels like years. Death ages people. Death quiets the rowdiness.

I've lived closely with death for a very long time. I dance with death in the sunlight and sleep in its embrace.

I look full and long into Landry's face. I feel like I've looked into those eyes for all time--the brown rimmed with green. His lashes are dark and thick, the liquid depth of his soul shining through.

His lips are full and sensuous, taunting me with kisses unkissed.

The color of his face, the light chocolate smoothness of it, offsets his beautifully-white teeth.

I sigh.

I could look at his face endlessly. And if not forever, for as long as I can get.

Because today I was reminded, once again, that life ends in a split second--that it's over in the time it takes to blink--that you're alive one minute and dead the next.

I'm reminded once again.

Chapter 11

The water is miraculous. The minerals transfer heat to my bones. I absorb it through my pores, letting the warmth radiate into my cells, feeling my body temperature raise.

The Hot Springs are a thousand feet lower than Leadville and that makes all the difference. The air temperature is fifteen degrees warmer and the gentle wind isn't tracking off high mountain snowfields.

I breathe the balmy air and lift my face to the sun as I float on my back, arms and legs weightless in the buoyancy of the water.

Landry has one hand on my back and one on my belly. I crave his touch until the end of time but I can't think of that right now. For now I want to suspend time the way the water is suspending me.

The sun is too bright to open my eyes so I don't. I float, safely between Landry's hands, absorbing the sun's rays. I feel like a block of ice thawing, melting from the edges inward. The hard crystals at my core bend and yield. I float and soften, eyes closed. Time does not matter right now.

Time is all I have, I think.

We leave the pool after dark. Although I've been careful, I'm still sunburned. It's a light burn, enough to break the Leadville frost layer that resides just beneath my skin.

We dress for dinner and eat well, asking for seconds and thirds on the bread basket. Laughter returns to our lives, tentatively and unsure of itself.

We call Clyde from the payphone in the lobby after a dessert of apple pie and ice cream.

"No news," he tells us.

"Quiet tonight," I say.

"Lot of people driving around."

"No one wants to be home," I say. No one ever wants to be home.

I know the town is once again frozen in death and violence. I'm glad to be here, in the softer, warmer darkness.

"Landry?" says Clyde suddenly.

"Yeah?" responds Landry, sharing the phone receiver with me.

"Good luck. You know—" Clyde means Vietnam, boot camp, all the uncertainty that life will be handing Landry with brutal nonchalance.

"Thanks, Clyde,"

There's nothing else to say. Nothing that words can cover. We listen to each other's silence and Landry hangs up the phone.

Landry and I return to our room. We make love slowly and gently, affirming life, affirming breath.

He smells of the pool and I lose myself in his scent. I bury my nose in his neck and I could breathe him infinitely. There's no sound but our pounding hearts. It's so quiet I can hear the stars expand.

Landry is exquisitely beautiful in the light reflecting through the drapes. His skin takes on a silver tone, making him look like a Greek god.

"You are beautiful," I tell him.

He smiles.

I touch his shoulders, his face, the curves of his waist and hips. We make love for hours, the heat of him inside me leading me through eclipsing tides of passion. I crest and slip into the lull of timelessness.

And it starts over again. I follow my body's moods, my body's responses to Landry.

It's weightless, drifting in an open sea. It's so easy, so fluid. I go with it, caught in a current of desire, letting rapture surge and ebb endlessly.

Chapter 12

We sleep, tangled limbs in the night. The warmth of his body permeates my dreams. He sighs and I moan.

The poolside motel is noiseless all night. The hush feels unusual to me. Most of the nights at the home of my childhood were interrupted by drunken arguments, heated discussions and the invariable crash of things being thrown.

The only thing I hear is Landry's breathing. We're in a deep sleep. Our refuge separates me from the world of craziness that has been my life. In Landry's arms, I sleep like I've never slept before.

I wake in his arms and find him, covering his mouth with mine, running my jaw along his cheek, biting his neck. I wake him with my desire. He meets my ardor, opening his arms to me. I take control of him. It feels powerful and tantalizing, being the aggressor, asking his body to reply when I take him into my mouth.

His skin is silky over his hardness. I explore his shape and the wideness of him. My tongue circles him, swirling his lust.

"Baby," he whispers.

I know I must be doing something right so I experiment with him, listening to the pace of his breathing, sensing the tightening of the muscles in his hips and belly.

He growls, low and deep in his chest. I feel my stomach clench and the fire starts between my legs. I run my nails down his chest and it's more than he can take.

He flips me onto my back before I know what has happened. His lips sear mine as he enters me. It's so different from last night. This morning is savage desire and animal lust. He can't get enough of me and the scorching hunger in him thrills the blood in my veins.

He pushes into me, slamming his hipbones on the inside of my thighs. I open my legs wider and wider still, giving him access to me. He takes it. He takes me.

"Baby," he says again. There's thickness in his voice, a delirium rumbling from his fever-pitch.

I grab his hair with both hands and pull his kiss harder against my lips. The heat of his tongue finds mine. There are no boundaries between us. No lines exist. No separation.

"Mmmmm," I moan.

Landry moves into me, finding me, feeling me. We're fiercely focused on each other because all the barriers are down. I feel my body launching into a frontier from the rhythm and earnestness of his sex.

He must sense the exploding change in me because he suddenly gets bigger and even harder.

"Maddie," he calls out.

It works in tandem, like we're setting each other off, a syncopation of beat and back-beat, a symphony fusing down to a single sound—my scream.

Chapter 13

Except for my giggling, which I can't control, breakfast is ethereal. My knees don't work right, my ankles are floppy and I feel like Olive Oyl—the loose-limbed, goofy companion of Popeye.

My state of kookiness makes Landry chuckle. He shakes his head each time I succumb to a new onslaught of hilarity. I can barely eat.

"Why does the food taste squeaky?" I ask Landry.

He laughs and I squeeze my eyes shut, relishing every second of this divine comedy.

"The air smells like colors! Purple is the strongest—lilacs, I think. Lilacs and velvet. Yellow smells like sunshine, did you know that?"

Landry spreads jelly on his toast and looks at me with a sparkling light in his glance that makes me wiggle my toes. I'm supremely happy. "I didn't know purple had a scent but it does," I tell him.

The day unfolds magically. We float in the pool and play in the river. The heated water bubbling from the streambed mixes enticingly with the ice melt flowing from the mountaintops. It dances deliciously over our bare feet and legs.

We hop in his car and take a drive to inspect the chalk cliffs. The chalk isn't really chalk.

"It's kaolinite," I tell him.

The soft rock is produced by hot springs percolating through cracks in the mountain. It's chalky and white and brittle, collapsing under our fingers as we make an ambiguous attempt to climb.

We eat lunch and go back to the room to make love. We savor each other's bodies. We laugh. I sing. He dances. We kiss deeply, suspended in time. We can't get enough of our nakedness. We make memories to last us.

We go out barefoot, finding a tree that has fallen across the stream. We lie along the length of its trunk, watching the dapples of sunlight on the underside of the log. I open myself.

There's no reason not to.

As the sun sets, we go out in the Camaro, to the place I logged in my mind from the earlier drive.

"Do it," Landry encourages.

I take down the clutch and set the wheels smoking as I find third gear and take the vehicle smoothly sideways through a set of curves inviting such adventure.

"So cool," he says.

I can't let him drive. It's not my car.

My brother Rusty donated the car to my cause and entrusted it to me while he's on a Navy carrier. He wrote that he's in the Mediterranean but I don't believe his words. I think he's in Vietnam.

I don't offer and Landry doesn't ask. He's impressed with the technique Rusty and I developed.

"We experimented first in snow-packed parking lots," I tell him. "We tried it on dirt. And then we took it to pavement."

It's a hyper-blown float above the surface, tires skidding as I play out gear ratio out in high-speed drift.

"Whoo!" Landry hoots and I join him.

It's fun. It's flashy and exciting. It's unharnessed speed and lightning-quick reflexes. It makes my pulse sprint and my heart thump and I love it.

The night is young and we decide to check out the drive-in movie theater at the edge of Buena Vista. I drive, too fast, into the night. Exhilaration has laid claim to us.

We arrive as the previews are starting. The main feature is *The Ballad of Cable Hogue* and we're excited to see it. We park in the back row and I hook the speaker onto the side window.

"Popcorn!" Landry launches himself from the car in search of buttery treats.

I lean back in the seat, breathing the softness of the air.

Mountain air is sharp and crisp, lacking voluptuousness. It's easy to breathe this air. It doesn't take the effort required at timberline.

The movie starts. We watch Jason Robards, betrayed by his partners and left to die in the desert. By the time he discovers the water hole that shapes the course of his life, I have my head on Landry's shoulder and we have devoured the popcorn.

I love the movie. It's quirky and sweet and funny and I watch Landry enjoying it out of the corner of my eye.

I love the cinema. I love surrendering to the magic, to the dissolving of reality, to being played--emotions tickled and heartstrings tugged. I want to do what Stella Stevens does—transform into someone else, perform a role so impeccably, so superbly, it's alchemical.

Landry knows I'm enthralled.

When the movie finishes, when Cable meets his end, Landry takes my face in his hands and looks into my eyes.

"You can do that," he tells me. "I know you can."

I look down.

He won't take no for an answer.

He repeats it. "I know you can. You have what it takes." He kisses me, pulling me to him.

I feel my body respond. The heat flashes between us. I tingle all the way down to my toes.

We make love all night, summoning the divine.

Chapter 14

I like being lost in Landry. I soothe my jagged edges in the warm, mineral-rich pool, basking with the sun in my face, weightless. It feels like another world, another planet. And it is. Buena Vista is as far removed from Leadville as Jupiter from Mercury.

When Landry touches me, when the heat of his hands is against my flesh, nothing else matters. I feel reborn, introduced to a new way of breathing, a new way of being.

I let myself fall into the buoyancy of being in love. I crave it but won't say it. I kiss him until the earth quakes. I give myself to him until the stars fall from the sky. It happens every time.

The words *I love you* pound in my head but I hold them back from my tongue. I refuse to say it. This feeling, this surging of emotion is mine and mine alone.

The smell of him, the taste of him is all that matters. We make love until we're drenched in each other, until hours pass and we must leave the room or risk dying there, of starvation or ecstasy, or both.

Driven from the bed, I drop coins into the payphone, calling Clyde first. Landry waits by the window, listening but not listening.

Clyde reports that nothing has changed with the search. No body has been found. The town is silent.

He asks, "Are you okay?"

"Landry is wonderful. I need this time."

"I understand. Do what you need to do, girl."

"I will."

Landry wanders over to speak to him for a few moments.

I feed more coins into the phone and call Steve's house. Eleanor, his mother, from whom all the kids inherited the deep, husky voice, answers. I know her from the children's plays. She works behind the scene on props and lights. Solid and fun, she's younger than can be possible after having eleven children. She tells me Steve is still asleep but knows he wants to talk to me. I tell her I will call later.

There's a silence as we hold the receivers, miles apart, not knowing what to say.

I finally ask, "How is everyone?"

"You know how it is after these things."

"Yeah." It doesn't seem like enough so I repeat it. "Yeah."

We say goodbye and I walk up behind Landry, running my hands up his arms to his shoulders. We look out over the pool and he asks, "Everything okay?"

"It's what happens."

"I know."

I wonder if he does know.

Each time the town goes quiet, as if holding its breath. We wonder who the beast will claim next. We ponder whether this death has quelled its blood-lust. And for how long.

But we know it's not enough. It's never enough. Leadville eats its young.

From my conversation with Clyde, I know Henry's mother has set the memorial service out in time. It might be for herself or it might be for her husband, who is still angry and full of blame. He wants to know who made the dare. No one is talking.

His anger hangs over the town. He cruises the avenue, looking for the culprit, thinking he can see the guilt in a face in a passing car.

The blood-lust will return. And the dangerous way we live our lives, in the face of it, guarantees another willing sacrifice. We dance at the edge of the pit, daring it, because to do otherwise would mean sitting in our living rooms in front of the TV, waiting to die another way. Better to dance in defiance than to huddle in fear. It's going to happen anyway.

So we dance.

Chapter 15

We wake on the last morning. We're spooned together, my back and bottom hooked into Landry's chest and belly. His arms are around me and I turn my head to him when I feel him move.

He kisses me and the world encompasses us, entwined in bed, searching for each other in the morning light.

His mouth is so confident, his lips setting the blood pumping through my body. Desire flares in me, hot and thick.

"I want you," he whispers, his breath damp on my neck.

I moan. It's all I can do when he touches me. He buries his fingers in my hair and passion pools in my belly, reaching lower to the wetness between my legs.

I want him as much as he hungers for me. My body's response feeds on his need for me. It's directly proportional.

He moves his body over mine, slowly, slowly, slowly lowering his weight onto me.

I can feel his heart beating against my breasts. His skin is sultry against mine. The warm smoothness of him tantalizes every cell in me. I squirm so I'm flat on my back, able to feel as much of his body as possible.

I slide my hands over the breadth of his back, tightening down into his hips and bottom, as inviting as the impending dawn.

"Landry," I savor his name on my tongue. Saying his name fills my head with whirling vapor.

"Madelyn," he murmurs and I can tell he's flush with me too.

I close my eyes and lift my arms over my head to lengthen the way my body touches his.

He lifts himself off me by pulling back onto his knees. He strokes me all the way down with slow, heavy hands--my face, along my neck, to my breasts and waist, pulling my hips down and opening my legs.

"Maddie," his voice rumbles deep from his chest.

I bite my lower lip, my teeth grazing the soft skin. The anticipation is delicious agony.

I feel his mouth on the inside of my thigh and I groan.

His tongue touches my flesh and I shudder. I raise myself on my elbows but he pushes me down, taking control of me. I let him. I want to abdicate to his desire, to the way he knows my body.

He takes the lips of my sex in his mouth and it triggers a shot of lightning that runs up through my scalp. I grab the sheets and hear myself keening, a sob elongating into the morning.

He moans his approval and the vibration sets up waves of pleasure that course along my spine.

I gasp for air but my lungs feel numb. I capture enough to keep living but I'm not sure I want to. The ecstasy of what he's doing drowns me in a sea of indulgence.

I'm powerless to do anything but feel what his mouth is doing, the movement, the slow repetition of his tongue.

I skid down the face of a wave and collapse into a place somewhere between space and time.

He holds still, perfectly still, the heat of his mouth excruciatingly luxurious. His hands grab my hips, pulling me down the bed to him. He enters me, hard and hot and stills again. I try to hold it off but my body takes me over the edge.

There's a sheen of sweat over me and I know he wants more. My body takes over, moving against him, asking for more, signaling my willingness, my readiness for him.

And he gives me what I was born a woman for— receiving his passion, his hunger, his maleness. We make love like it's our last, like we'll never touch again, like tomorrow won't come.

I give and give to him and he takes me, slaking his thirst for all that I am. He buries himself in me, over and over again, and I meet him there.

Like a tropical storm we crash together through every boundary, knocking down everything in our path. We light it on fire, the detonation in our heads and our bodies blowing it all to the heavens.

He will never forget me.

Never.

Chapter 16

Breakfast is quiet. Nothing tastes right. The eggs have a metallic flavor. The bacon tastes flat and subdued. The orange juice lacks luster.

The Marines have a pull on Landry now. His attention is elsewhere.

He will leave here and drive back to Pueblo. Saying goodbye to his family and returning his mother's car keys to her, he will board a bus with a duffle bag and report to San Diego. Thirteen weeks of boot camp will follow. His orders will come down. By all accounts, they'll be for Vietnam.

My life is taking a different direction. Next week I start my summer job at the Tabor Opera House. In the fall I'll begin classes at Colorado State University--unless, unless, unless I get the response I'm waiting for. I have other irons in the fire.

My brother, Rusty, on a Navy ship somewhere, should be the recipient of a letter telling him of my alternate design on life. Other than the missive to Rusty, no one knows about the letters to agents and acting companies. I haven't told my friends. My parents have no clue. I don't think I've even mentioned CSU to them.

I have a full scholarship waiting for me at the university. Francie Wilbur, my English and theater teacher, coordinated the recommendations to the drama department. I have to audition when I arrive, if I arrive, in the fall. I will do *Meteor Shower*, the play Francie wrote for me. Landry watched me perform it at the senior talent show on Saturday night.

Saturday night was long ago. Saturday was before Landry and I made love in the ballroom of the Opera House; before the storm washed through the valley, dancing fire across the mountain tops; before Henry Dill drowned in Twin Lakes; before Landry and I ran away to Mount Princeton Hot Springs and wrapped ourselves in warm water and warm sheets.

"It's only Wednesday," I say.

"Wednesday," repeats Landry quietly.

It has always been this way for me--a high-speed luge down the fall line of life--banking corners with the wind in my ears at every turn. But there's no stopping.

It's all been so terrifying that terror feels like home. It's the only thing I know. It's about violence and uncertainty and going on living when you don't know whether your brothers are alive or dead.

It's about growing up in the intangible, nothing certain, nothing sure. I guess at everything.

We dive into the pool and this time we swim, hard and competitively. We come off the wall in race starts.

"Come on!" Landry shouts.

We shoot across the pool and swim like our lives depend on it. Maybe they do.

Our legs shaky from the exertion, we return to the room and pack up, showering off the minerals and standing in front of each other.

He holds out his arms to me and I slide into his embrace effortlessly. He kisses me deeply, slowly, holding me tightly. He feels sublime. I'm caught up in the strength of his arms, the solid massiveness of his chest.

If I could seize a moment in time and hold it forever--capture it in a glass--this would be it.

Landry pulls his head back to say something.

That's when I realize, like the clanging of a bell, that I don't want to hear it. It doesn't matter what it is. I don't want to hear it.

I put my finger to his lips and quietly say, "Shhh."

I reach for my bag, walk out of the room, get in the Camaro and drive away.

Chapter 17

I'm going too fast but I'm afraid to slow down. I'm listening to Led Zeppelin at full volume. I want more and I know I can't have it--of Landry, of life, of feeling safe. I need a plan and I don't know what it is. I'm bereft. I try to hold on to my anger.

"I need a plan," I say out loud.

I smell Landry on my skin. I feel his mouth on me.

I need a plan. I'm moving so fast I catch air over the dips north of Buena Vista. I'm watching for deer. I need a plan.

If I had the ability to cry, I probably would. But that skill went away many years ago. I'm holding myself together because if I slip even a little, I might fly apart.

"I need a plan."

I see a hawk in flight over the road. I know it's an omen that everything will be all right. But I don't believe it. I can't believe it. The only thing I can believe right now is the speed at which I'm covering this road. I trust this car, the beautiful red Camaro. I trust her with my life.

The Arkansas River snakes along the highway to my right. The road follows it up to Climax, the molybdenum mine. At Climax, it's a small stream, the headwaters of the great river that flows into the Gulf of Mexico.

On the road at Buena Vista, the watercourse is wide and shallow. I see men fishing in waders, trying to catch the elusive, pink-fleshed rainbow trout. Most are fly-fishing, whipping their rods and flipping the fly across the surface of the water.

Jimmy Page rips across the song, *How Many More Times*. "Well, they call me a hunter, that's my name," sings Robert Plant.

I steer sideways into the curves. I know I shouldn't but I do it anyway. I take the Camaro down a gear and let out the clutch to smoke the tires. The adrenaline rush ramps it up. I keep the car in my lane as much as possible but we're sideways.

I'm playing chicken with the unknown. I cannot see around the curves and I don't care. The RPMs scream and the engine bites back. I want flight and she gives it to me. The wheels skim the pavement. I burn out rubber from the tires, leaving a trail of my anger for all to see.

It's then I realize I'm screaming.

My hands are firmly in control of the steering wheel. It's the key to the maneuver. I bring her around a curve in the opposite direction, sliding past the mile markers, the tires smoking.

I see another hawk above me--my totem animal.

Two hawks. I need to believe. I know I need to believe. I know I need to take my foot off the gas. I know I need to stop screaming.

Just a little more. Give me just a little more to make the anger back off, to appease the demons, to feed the monster.

I come up on the Granite General Store doing 120 miles per hour and I see my plan.

Chapter 18

I slide sideways into the parking lot, stopping short at the gas pump. I fill up the Camaro and go inside.

As I pass the grizzled man at the cash register, he raises an eyebrow at me. "A little fast there, don't you think?"

"Yeah." I admit. "A little fast."

I gather food for three days--jerky, potato chips, Cheerios and milk. I find cans of peas, apple sauce and pineapple to round it out.

"Do you know how far up Lost Canyon the road is open?" I ask.

"They haven't been in with the plow so not much past the last ranch on the flats, I imagine."

I thank him.

"Miss?" he intones. "Tad slower?"

I nod.

Like hell.

I point the Camaro up the dirt road behind the store. I'm going on a walkabout. I can't go back to Leadville yet. They'll have to understand.

It's not like I haven't done this before-- disappeared into the mountains, coming back days later. I have a knife. I have matches. I know how to survive.

We're not the clueless flatlanders who come up and wander away from camp in shorts and t-shirt, requiring rescue or burial. It's not Disneyland. The bears and mountain lions are real. Three feet of snow in June is real. The ride doesn't stop because someone freaks out. You know what you're doing or you die.

"It's as simple as that," I say.

I roll down the window to breathe in the spring air, the scent laced with sagebrush.

"Landry," I like the sound of his name on my tongue.

I've spent three days in paradise with him and I'm not ready for reentry into the cold bitterness of my hometown.

"Not yet," I tell myself.

I have a few more days before the Opera House opens for the season.

The snow is deep and unplowed once I get past the ranches. I make it as far as I can, to the switchback at the old mine buildings. I set up camp.

I start a fire in the woodstove and hang my provisions, checking to ensure I can secure the door against predators, both human and otherwise. I fill the water tank in the stove with snow to melt as the stove heats up. I sit outside on a broken chair to watch the sparkles of sunlight refract through my damp eyelashes.

I hear a pika chirping at me from a rock ledge. I watch a ground squirrel collecting food for a new litter she has hidden somewhere. I listen for birdcalls but it's still too early.

The stream trickles down beside the cabin, bubbling with snowmelt. I need to hollow out a cache to act as a reservoir.

I think about staying forever, disappearing into the mountains and giving in to mental illness without a fight--talking to myself and freezing to death this winter in the shape of a cross. Like Baby Doe.

Chapter 19

I sleep away the afternoon into the night. I get up to add wood to the fire so the freezing temperatures don't finish me in my exhausted emotional state. I bring in water from the stream because the snow I scooped into the stove boiled down to a few tablespoons. The sleeping bag is subzero but I don't want to breathe ice crystals at night.

"It's too hard on the lungs," I announce to the walls.

I lie on the cot and watch the auroras dance on the ceiling. Scientists say they're not northern lights, that we're too far south, but we know better. We have been watching them all our lives. Their iridescent halos mesmerizing in reflection, I sleep and wake and sleep again.

I don't hear bears and have seen no fresh scat. The camp doesn't have the strong scent of bear either. They must still be denning.

I dream of Landry.

When dawn breaks, the cabin is cold despite the warm ashes in the stove. I stoke it and add wood, hopping back into my sleeping bag to make morning manageable.

"Little brisk," I shiver.

For the next three days I go on walkabout in the dewy, thaw-soaked forest, winding my way among snow drifts.

"Kinnikinnick," I say, identifying the evergreen shrub that will produce pink flowers later this month, in anticipation of the berries in the fall.

I allow thoughts of Landry to float through my mind and I relish them. I don't try to hold them or push them out. He's a part of me. The memories will find me for the rest of my life, as if gently touching my shoulder. I know that.

"I welcome it," I tell the forest.

I want everything from Landry. And I want nothing from Landry. I don't want him to feel pressured. I want him to remember me the way I'm remembering him, as a gift, as an angel who dropped in for a few days to say hi, change my life, love me and leave.

I love the way my body aches for him. It's a new sensation and my body has felt many new sensations in the last week.

I know the heat of his tongue, the electric response that shoots through me, the presence of him inside me, hard and desirous.

I remember the splendor of his shoulders, the smoothness of his hips, the strength of his arms.

I will not jeopardize the pristine memories by pursuing awkward phone calls and tentative letters--the dissonance of forced contact. I don't want him to feel the need for follow-up.

"I'll be fine." I declare.

Two hawks confirmed it.

I stand still when I notice fog rising from the reservoir in the valley below. It rolls toward me up the mountain, like a cloud on wheels, glistening and wet. As it climbs over the meadow below me, I feel the cold dampness preceding it. Rolling over on itself from top to bottom, it catches footholds on the mountain.

My heart stops as it enfolds me, surrounding me in a thick glassiness that obliterates everything except its wisps and vapors. It rolls on past, through me, up to the peak where it joins the clouds in the sky.

I spend my time on walkabout breathing the air, singing the songs in my head and remembering Landry.

I think about my brothers, Rusty and Joel, and wonder where they are. I stretch out my hands to feel them but there's only oblivion. I strain to hear an answer on the wind but there's nothing.

Chapter 20

I drive back to Leadville on Saturday. I'm calm. I have considered a lot of things, not deeply or well, but that's okay.

"It's going to have to be," I say, steering the rumbling Camaro onto Harrison Avenue.

I don't have any more plans. I used up the one that came to me in Granite—escaping to Lost Canyon.

I check my post office box with expectation but it's empty. There's nothing from Rusty.

Nothing from the theater companies or agents who have my head shots. No response to my putting myself out there, hoping, hoping I would be the one they pick, for whatever reason.

"Maybe the hawks are wrong," I mutter to myself.

I drive to Francie's house. She's cool with my using her number for important messages. She doesn't know it but it's her number on my head shots.

I ring the doorbell.

She swings the door open with her great strength.

When she sees it's me, she pulls me into a bear hug. "Maddie, come in, come in," she gushes.

I love her welcomes. She's effusive and grand and dramatic.

We go to the kitchen and she puts on water for tea.

"Do you know about Henry?" she asks.

I nod. "Yeah."

"That's right," she says. "I heard you went out to the lake."

"I went."

"Seems you said all the right things to those kids."

"I did?"

"I talked to a lot of them. Whatever you said was the right thing," she says, reaching for teabags in her cupboard.

"I don't remember what I said."

"And then you vanished. Again, I might add."

"Another walkabout," I admit.

There were a couple calls for you."

"Who?" I ask a little too brightly.

"Clyde for one. And I'm trying to remember--." She reaches for a stack of notes by her phone.

"Tina. Oh, Tina Lambrecht!" she exclaims.

"She teaches at the elementary school?

Francie nods. "She applied for a graduate program at the University of Iowa. Didn't get accepted—waitlisted. This week an opening came up and she grabbed it and took off. She asked me to watch her house and her cat. Water the plants."

I nod.

"But the cat's getting weird without anyone there. Tina called to check and I told her the cat is going psycho. She asked if I knew anybody who could stay there for the summer. I thought of you."

"What?" I gasp.

A place to live. I run out of oxygen and the room starts to spin.

I can't believe it. This is what the hawks were foretelling--that I would find a home.

I'm so excited, we leave our tea unfinished on the kitchen table and jump in the Camaro. I follow Francie's directions to Eleventh Street and there it is–a little Victorian dollhouse, complete with a miniature porch and gingerbread trim.

Francie unlocks the door and we walk into a book-filled cottage with flocked wallpaper and antique furniture. The windows are beveled glass and the curtains are rich velvet.

I fall in love with the place. Francie looks at me expectantly. I melt into her arms again.

"It's-- It's—" I stammer.

"It is, isn't it?" she laughs.

I see soft inquisitive eyes under the couch and ask, "Is that--?"

"Jethro. He's a little shy but he'll get used to you. I'll show you the instructions now that you're so graciously taking over."

Francie is the gracious one. This means the world to me and she knows it but pretends not to. She acts like I'm the one doing her a favor. I love her in this moment like I have never loved her before.

"How soon can you--?"

"Now," I interrupt.

Francie raises an eyebrow and laughs.

"Good," she says.

Chapter 21

I edge the nose of the Camaro around the corner of Mount Princeton Drive. I cannot count the times I have done this, sneaking up on my own house, attempting to gauge if it's safe to enter.

There are no cars parked in the driveway. My mother is doing her waitressing shift at the Golden Burro. I'm more concerned about seeing my father's Jeep.

"Cool," I say, seeing the Jeep is gone also.

I don't know where he is but I have this opportunity to get my belongings out, once and for all.

I park in the driveway and slip in the front door, listening for a moment. My senses are on high alert. I hear nothing but the clock ticking in the kitchen.

I grab garbage bags from under the kitchen sink and stuff all my clothes from the bedroom closet in two of them. I repeat the process with my dresser, raking things from the drawers and stuffing everything into a bag.

I wonder if my parents have broken up again. Maybe. Maybe not. It changes hour-by-hour with them.

I clear the shelves of my photo albums and books and retrieve the box of diaries from under the bed.

My farewell ritual is tearing all the posters from the wall and stuffing them in the garbage can. I even trash the *Keep On Truckin'* poster from Zap magazine.

"My time here is over," I announce.

I open the door to the room that housed my brothers, Rusty and Joel, a long time ago. The door is always closed and the room is a shrine. Joel's baseball trophies line the head of his bed. His skis and boots, topped with his racing jersey, lean into the corner. He left behind a cold-case file, a million memories and several hundred broken hearts.

Across the room is Rusty's bed. His basketball trophies adorn the bookshelf. His sash for winning the Mr. Legs contest in high school is draped over his golf clubs and track cleats.

Rusty lived in this shrine for three years before he graduated from high school and bailed into the Navy.

Every time he opened the closet door, Joel's shirts and jeans hung beside his own. Joel's clothes hang there still.

Rusty cleaned out his half when he left for the service. It was his farewell.

The Camaro was his promise to me. He promised he would not die in Vietnam.

The last time he was home on leave, the changes in him were conspicuous. The war was gnawing on him like a rat. Neither of us spoke of the future. We're trying to survive the day, one hour, one step, at a time. We're using all our effort to stay alive.

We talked about the weather.

I wade to the front door through the flotsam and jetsam of my parents' destruction, carrying bags and the box of diaries. The television still has a hole through the screen. Another lamp has been broken. The holes punched in the walls cannot be counted.

I load everything into the trunk and slam the lid as my father drives up. He steps out and slams the door behind him, a scowl on his face.

My blood runs cold.

"Where the hell have you been?" he asks.

"Lost Canyon," I reply, scowling back.

"You don't even know what happened," he accuses.

"What happened?" I ask, hard and cold.

"That Dill boy drowned. Parents are a mess. And you--you're off gallivanting around. Don't care about your friends. Don't care about the Dill family. Just like you, taking off when there's trouble. Don't care about nobody but yourself. Selfish bitch."

I stare him down, saying nothing.

"Why don't you pack your fucking bags and get out," he spits, taking a threatening step toward me.

I back away and reach for the door handle. The button under my thumb sends a spiral of anger through me.

"Watch me," I say, stepping into the Camaro, slamming the door and driving away.

And just like that, I'm gone.

Chapter 22

I unlock the door to Tina's house, my house, with the key. I carry everything in from the car and drop it inside the front door. I turn the deadbolt and sink to the floor.

I breathe. I close my eyes. I listen and there isn't a sound. I open my eyes and see clean, gentle surroundings. I don't want to stir. I run my fingers along the wood floor on which I'm sitting, my back leaning against the door.

Even though I'm only eighteen, I feel decades younger than I did five minutes ago. I feel buoyant. Living here will be elegant.

"I'm not a hummer. I don't hum," I announce to the cat, wherever he is.

I'm sure he's watching me but I can't see his pretty little eyes anywhere.

I don't know what he makes of the stranger sitting on the floor inside his front door next to a pile of garbage bags. I'm sure he's never seen anything quite like it. I doubt Tina has ever collapsed on the floor in a heap of quiet gratitude.

"Kitty, kitty," I call softly. "Here, Jethro."

He does not appear. I rise from the floor and begin unpacking with slow, deliberate movements. I won't scare him if he doesn't scare me. We will go easy with this.

There's plenty of space in the closet to hang my clothes. I find empty cardboard boxes on the back porch and build a bookshelf and dresser with them.

I whisper to myself, "I live here now. I live here now. I live here now."

It's a delicious mantra. The repetition helps me believe it.

There are only five rooms but I find myself wandering through the house, touching the gleaming surfaces. I luxuriate in the thickness of the rugs beneath my feet.

"Tea?" I ask Jethro, an open invitation. I put on the teapot and sit at the kitchen table staring out the window.

I take a bath in the deep tub because I've been camping for three days and know I smell like it. The steam from the hot water engulfs me and I breathe it in silence.

I relax into the weight of the water, knowing that no chaos is going to explode through the front door. I can't believe my good fortune.

"I never want to leave," I tell Jethro.

I soak for two hours, using my toes to turn on the hot water. I keep the temperature so hot it's almost unbearable. I sink into a drowsiness that is deep and still. I fall asleep half a dozen times but the line between waking and sleeping is tenuous and blurred.

At one point, Jethro pokes his pixie face around the corner of the doorway.

"Hi," I say.

He retreats quickly when our eyes meet.

"Jethro," I call but he does not reappear.

Fluffy towels greet me when I pull the stopper and stand up in the tub. They are so white, they gleam. I pull one around my body, appreciating the humor of being enthralled by a towel. I wrap my long hair in the other towel and step out of the tub.

I make up the bed with sheets I find ironed and folded in the closet. I pull a comforter over the bed and crawl in, clean and naked.

I sleep the sleep of the dead.

Chapter 23

I sleep through the night. I wake at dawn on Sunday morning after fifteen hours of slumber.

When I roll over to stretch, I see Jethro sitting on the blanket chest looking at me. This time he doesn't run. Maybe he's been watching me all night. If so, he probably thinks I died. I'm sure I didn't move.

"Hello, little buddy," I say to him.

He doesn't answer but he's no longer frightened. He's content to watch me with five feet of space between us. I know his serenity would change if I reached for him so I don't.

"I forgot to feed you last night, didn't I?" I ask guiltily.

Since that is obviously the case, I'm impressed he's not complaining.

I move slowly out of bed and open a can of wet cat food, adding it to some dry kibble for his bowl. I refresh the water for him.

"There you go. Better? Forgive me?" I ask soothingly.

While Jethro eats, I jump in the shower. I can't get enough. The warm water runs in rivulets down my body and through my hair, washing away the sleep. I shampoo and condition my hair, using Tina's Prell. I make a mental note to start a list so I can replace what I use.

"Thank you, Tina," I whisper under the showerhead. I don't know how she has limitless hot water, which apparently is the case. The gods are smiling on me.

Jethro waits for me in the doorway when I turn off the water.

"Did you finish your breakfast?" I ask him. "I hope I made it to your satisfaction. I truly apologize for starving you last night. It won't happen again, I promise."

After I dry off with Tina's million-dollar towels, I dress and wander into the kitchen. The cat isn't the only one starving.

Tina has not left much in the way of food. Her pantry is spare, dwindled down because she thought the house would be empty for the summer.

"Cheerios," I announce to Jethro, remembering the camping supplies still in the car.

I steel myself to unlock the front door and run outside into the real world to retrieve breakfast. My bare feet hit the cold sidewalk and I make the round trip speedily and suspiciously. I haven't thought about who lives on this block and I don't want to deal with anyone. I slam and lock the door behind me.

"Safe!" I yell triumphantly.

Jethro follows me into the kitchen and I brew tea, which I drink at the table, eating Cheerios straight from the box. I find a notebook and begin a grocery list.

I turn the page and start a letter to Rusty, telling him of the fortune that has befallen me. I describe the house, right down to the velvet curtains. Neither of us has lived in a place even remotely like this. I tell him about the patina of the floors, the attention to detail, the antique furniture and the absurdly-thick towels.

Even before Joel disappeared, our family home was always knee-deep in clutter. Any flat surface was piled with paperwork, old cereal bowls and fast-food wrappers.

In the letter I tell Rusty I'm going to cook. I picture myself cooking. I run my fingers along the cookbooks placed neatly on the shelf beside the table.

I will sit at this lovely kitchen table and look out on the quiet backyard and eat slowly and calmly. I will go to bed at night knowing I'm protected from the outside world.

I will soak forever in the tub.

I will live.

Chapter 24

When I finish the letter to Rusty, I sit in silence. I try to generate a connection with him, a trick we established many years ago.

I call in Joel while I'm at it. There's a chance, I know there's a chance, that he's out there, somewhere, alive, thinking of me.

I surround my brothers with a field of energy-- shimmering silver--and I open it a little more to include Landry.

"Landry," I say.

Beautiful, sensual Landry.

I don't know where a single one of them is. I blow out a slow exhale to protect them and keep them safe, conveying that I hold them in my heart. It's a message on the wind.

I hear a meow.

"Jethro," I sing to the cat. "Jethro the Jaguar."

He likes it, watching me attentively.

I reach for the phone by the table. I should lift the receiver from the hook. I can make outgoing calls. Incoming calls go to Tina's answering machine where she can listen to them remotely.

"No," I sigh, taking my hand away. I make another cup of tea instead.

When I call Steve an hour later, he sounds flattened and whipped. Not much has changed. They have discontinued the search. No resolution. No closure--just a bunch of people sitting around Dunn's Bar every night looking at each other over beer.

I tell him I've left home and am house-sitting. I don't give him the details and he lets it go.

He tells me, "I miss seeing you."

He starts work at the mine on Monday.

"We'll get together soon," I say.

There's silence. There's nothing more to say but it feels good to sit on the phone with him. Sometimes things don't need to be said.

When we hang up, I gather my dirty clothes and read the instructions for the washing machine. I stand with the lid open, watching the water rush into the tub. When the agitator starts, I jump, shaken from my reverie.

Leadville is quicksand. I've been back twenty-four hours and I can feel it sucking around my ankles. It pulls at me, drawing me down into bogginess, wet and spongy. There's a price to be paid for living here. The place ensnares, like Henry caught in the weeds and the muck at the bottom of the lake.

After a while, you stop fighting it.

Chapter 25

I can't.

I can't make the calls. I sit with my hand on the receiver but I'm unable to lift it again.

I can't bring myself to go out either. It's Leadville out there—ramped-up craziness that never stops. It goes on and on, day and night. It's as constant as the wind buffeting the mountains, as eternal as the clouds scudding overhead.

I'll continue scavenging for food today so I don't have to go out. I'll raid what's left of Tina's pantry.

"Hello, baby," I coo to the cat, who watches me with infinite patience.

I wander the house, mine for the summer. I leaf through cookbooks, imagining. I run my fingers over the linens and towels in the closet. I lie on the bed transfixed by the way Tina has pulled back decades of wallpaper strips to produce an intimate history of the house.

"Jethro, sweetest kitty," I sing to him as the sun sets orange and violet on the western peaks.

I scoop his food into a bowl and wander toward the bathroom where I soak in another endless bath.

In sleep, I dream of my brother, Rusty. I stand outside on a sidewalk, peering through a window at him. He's happy, sitting in a small cafe and looking into the eyes of a woman I don't recognize. She has dark hair and eyes like his. She laughs and pours wine into his glass.

I don't want to interrupt. I smile at the light dancing in his eyes.

He pulls a chunk of bread from a long loaf and feeds it to the woman. I cannot hear what they are saying. He looks so young and handsome in his Navy uniform.

I'm witness to the kiss he places on her lips, leaning across the table. The woman puts her hand to his face and pulls him toward her. He whispers something. She kisses him back.

"Oh," I sigh and Rusty turns as if he has heard.

He looks directly at me and suddenly the dream recedes. Rusty reaches out to me and I put my palm against the window. He says something but I can't hear it.

"What?" I shout as they shrink into the distance.

"What?" I yell but they're gone.

I've lost them. I turn over, happy with the glimpse of them.

The rest of the night is given over to dreams of Landry. I feel the warmth of him like bubbles against my flesh. I sense his breath on my breasts, his lips on my neck. His hands drift lazily across the small of my back and he murmurs low and slow until I wake up.

I open my eyes to Jethro, staring at me from the blanket chest.

"Hi," I say to him.

He does not answer.

Chapter 26

"How many summers with me, Maddie?" asks Evelyn Furman, the owner of the Opera House, when I report for my summer job.

"Five," I confirm.

"You know as much about this place as I do."

"I doubt that."

Evelyn Furman knows more about this building than anyone on earth. She lives and breathes the Opera House, its history and secrets.

"The new girls are here," she says, motioning me into the appliance store she runs on the ground floor.

I follow and look over Evelyn's recruits. They are young, all going into ninth grade. She hires them young so she can keep them every summer during high school.

"This is Nancy, Nell and Nora," she says quickly.

I raise an eyebrow. "Three N's?"

"That's what we'll call them!"

"Okay, who's who?" I ask the girls.

"I'm Nora," volunteers the girl with glasses and braces.

"Nancy" is claimed by the lovely Hispanic girl, the depth of her eyes bottomless.

"And you must be Nell," I say to the remaining one, who nods her tumble of brown curls.

They look at each other and giggle nervously.

"I'll leave you to it," says Evelyn, returning to her desk.

I lead the Three N's up the grand staircase to the theater and sit them in the front row so they'll be comfortable while I start their training.

"The Tabor Opera House was built in 1879 by Horace Austin Warner Tabor—called HAW or H.A.W. for short. He and his wife Augusta were shopkeepers. HAW loved to grubstake prospectors, which Augusta hated, but it paid off for him in 1877 when the Little Pittsburgh..."

The girls pay attention, trying to make a good impression but also because it's a story of gold, riches, adultery, divorce, scandal, failure and ruin—and who doesn't like those stories?

I wander with them through the magnificent structure, continuing the history lesson and climbing all the staircases to make sure they are thoroughly lost but impressed by the grandeur of the old girl.

"The walls need paint, the floors need tile, the ceiling in the attic is caving in but she's a treasure and Evelyn does the best she can," I explain to them.

Nora talks the most, asking questions and saying, "Groovy," every time she spots something noteworthy—the dusty chandeliers, the brass fittings, the antique sinks, the oil lamps, the actors' trunks.

I point out the barred doors that open into the air three stories above the alley—where the walkway to the Clarendon Hotel existed decades ago.

When I walk them through the ballroom, I pause by the bed where Landry and I made love, light-headed and lost in memories.

"Oooh," the girls croon over the elegance and cob-webbed grandeur of the place.

"I saved the best for last," I tell them, switching on the light board by the stage. I watch the girls dance under the brightness.

Before I hand out the scripts to memorize, we make a stop in the costume room to paw through the beautiful old gowns. We hold them up to see what fits, what needs repair, figuring out how to make the girls look like they stepped out of the 1880s.

We dissolve into giggles. I feel centuries older than they are.

They are lovely girls, sweet and sarcastic and bright. It's going to be a lively summer.

Chapter 27

I lock up the Opera House and walk to my car where Landry once caught me and kissed me and set my world on fire. It seems like a million years ago.

Clyde drives up. He's prowling the alley looking for my car, I can tell. He rolls down the window.

"Hi," he says.

"Hi," I say back.

"Did you start work today?"

"Training. Three girls."

"Great," he says. "I started work at the mine. Safety training. We won't be going underground until next week." There's a pause. "Do you want to get something to eat?"

"Yeah."

I get in his car and we drive to the J-Mar, finding a booth and settling in.

Margaret takes our order. When she leaves, we sit looking at our hands. There's a distance I've never felt with Clyde before.

"Did Landry make it to San Diego?" I ask.

"Yup. He's been calling. Asking about you. I didn't know where you were."

"I know. I'm sorry."

"I couldn't find you or Bette,"

"I think she ran off to get married."

He laughs and grows quiet again. "What are we doing, Maddie?"

"I don't think we know."

"I know I don't."

"Me neither." I look out the window and watch people going into Sayer-McKee Drugs.

"Are we dying?" he asks suddenly.

"Fast or slow, I guess we are."

"Do you want Landry to call?"

"I don't know."

"What should I tell him?"

I pause. I don't know what I want. I long for Landry. I crave him. But hearing his voice again, the gentle rumbling of it, would unravel me.

I reach for a napkin and scribble a number.

"He can write. I'll give you my box number. I don't have a phone. I found a place. Or Francie found me a place, I should say."

"You left home?"

"Moved out. House-sitting for Tina Lambrecht. Little dream house."

"I'm glad," he says. "Me and some of the guys are renting a house. I was going to invite you but I guess you're set up."

"Tina's place is good. It's more than good."

"How did you leave it with your parents?"

"I just left. There wasn't anything to say. How is it with your parents?"

"My dad says I'm a man now. Mom's been sewing curtains and giving me her extra plates."

We laugh. I wonder what it would be like, having parents who care.

"I'm glad you're out of there," he says.

"Yeah. Me, too."

The food arrives and we eat in silence. It tastes good and I'm hungry.

I can tell he's preoccupied with going underground.

I sit across the table from him and I can smell his doubt and fear. I wonder if he can smell it on me.

It hangs heavy in the air. It's cold and wet. Like Henry, trapped and dead at the bottom of Twin Lakes.

Chapter 28

Clyde and I promise to get together again soon. I tell him I will cook for him at my new place. He invites me to his housewarming party when they get moved in, some weeks down the line.

He drops me off at my car and drives away after a long hug. We don't know what else to say. I watch him drive off and even the air feels different.

I park the Camaro at Super Foods. I live a hundred yards away. I will be able to walk here and carry home fresh vegetables, sweet-smelling fruit, gallons of cold milk, whenever I want.

Right now I'm going to shop big. I'm stocking up the pantry, luxuriating in the feel and smell of the food I load into the cart.

I drive it all home and pile the paper bags on the kitchen table, locking the door behind me and calling out to the cat. I fill the refrigerator and the pantry shelves.

"Food, food, food," I sing.

Food like I've never had before. I will eat and I will eat well.

When done, I sit at the table and open the *Joy of Cooking* to Page One.

After an amazing dinner of lambs chops and mint jelly with a heaping fresh salad, I draw another extravagant bath and go to bed.

"Good night, Rusty. Sleep tight, Joel. Sweet dreams, Landry," I whisper, pulling the blankets around my chin.

I dream of Landry. I dream of Landry every night. I can feel his hands on me. I can smell the vaguely smoky scent of him. I remember the taste of his mouth. I think about the way my body responded to him, to his desire for me, to his beckoning of my body.

The intimacy carved our initials into my heart. Our sexuality had a savage elegance.

I wanted him and he wanted me. We surrendered to it.

"How could it ever be that way again? How could we talk on the phone or mail words to each other that wouldn't strip away everything?" I ask the cat.

He doesn't answer.

I lie in the coziness of the bed, looking at the ceiling pondering how Clyde asked what he should tell Landry.

"I don't know," I had finally answered.

Because I don't.

Landry and I moved earth and sky. We exploded solar systems. We broke apart our separate boundaries and found each other in an endless pool of melting passion.

"How can reality compete with that?" I turn to Jethro again.

He blinks.

I wake every morning longing for Landry but I don't know if I want anything more than that.

The longing is so pure.

I don't know where Landry is with any of this emotionally. I'm not sure I want to know. I want to believe he felt what I felt. But I'm not brave enough to risk hearing that he didn't. I don't want to listen to him stumble over awkward words. I don't want the intensity deflated in any way.

I want to hold it perfectly preserved and untainted—like a pressed corsage. I know it's selfish and cowardly of me.

I know he's in a place where he could use a friend. But I can't be that for him—a friend. I need what happened between us to be ethereal and otherworldly.

I would rather it be lovely and lost than take the gamble that it was less for him.

And I know boot camp is stamping its imprint into his soul.

Chapter 29

June ushers in alpine summer. The air warms and the sky softens, twinkling fairy lights at night. Summer is the magic season in the mountains.

Storms may blow in but they bring snow that won't stay. It will melt and be gone within days, watering the tentative green of the forest and making life a little less savage.

The Opera House girls, the Three N's, work out beautifully. They arrive in the morning, bubbly and personable, changing into their costumes, flirting with the tourists. The tip jar is always full. The money is welcome.

I return my graduation gown after I retrieve it from the back seat of the Camaro. It bore witness to many events in my life--covering my nakedness at a ceremony where I chose to wear nothing underneath, in open rebellion.

It lay as it was thrown as I tore up Fifth Street to the Diamond head frame, rested peacefully as I performed *Meteor Shower* at the talent show, slept through the transformative night I spent in the recesses of the Opera House with Landry, waited patiently as I escaped to the Hot Springs for three days of profound intimacy with Landry, followed by my walkabout at Lost Canyon.

I left it there, crumpled in the back seat, when I moved into Tina's house, leaving home and not looking back. It waited patiently to be returned to the high school to be placed in crates with the others.

For the first time in my life, I like going home. I can't wait to go home. Home is now a little house on Eleventh Street with a cat named Jethro. It's a new and wondrous experience for me.

One night Jethro jumps into my lap. I slowly scratch him under the chin. With that, we turn a corner and he begins to greet me at the door, follow me around the house, lounge on my legs and sleep at the bottom of the bed. He's charming company. I talk to him endlessly about whatever thoughts cross my mind.

He listens and makes no protest.

I have Clyde over for dinner and he's duly impressed with my cooking and the atmosphere.

"This is a good place, isn't it?" he observes. "This is the kind of place you belong."

I nod solemnly. He knows how it's been for me.

The town buries Henry, finally, when his parents allow it. The casket contains a picture, his senior picture. I attend, along with the rest of the town.

Everyone is still tight-lipped about who made the dare that sent Henry into the water.

His father glowers at all of us through the service, his hard eyes seeking a culprit to blame for his son's demise. He does not want to admit a bigger picture--his own culpability in producing a son who was as angry, hard-bitten and aggressive as he is--a young man incomplete enough to take a dare that would end his life.

Henry's mother sits beside her husband in the first row, hands clasped in her lap, her face old and grief-stricken. Henry's sisters sit beside her, using her as a shield from their father's rage. They are tearful and bereft.

I find a seat beside Steve Wadsworth and hold his hand.

"Bette's not here," whispers Steve.

I see Bette once at Food Town. I block her cart with mine and give her a hug. She talks too fast, nervously.

"It's wonderful being married," she gushes. "We have a little house near my mother's. A block from the old battle-axe. But it's the cutest place! I don't have a phone or car so I'm kind of stuck there."

I see flat heaviness in her eyes.

Her dimples dance. "I'll ask Danny if it's okay if you come by. He's waiting in the car. I told him I'd be right out."

Her pregnancy is showing, pronounced because she's so short.

I know I won't hear from her. She knows it too.

I stop by Francie's house regularly to report on the condition of the house and Jethro. I break down and tell her about the head shots.

She disapproves. She wants me to go to college but is cautiously optimistic for me, understanding my dreams because they were once hers.

I take dreamy drives in the Camaro, sometimes setting her down into a controlled skid but usually driving the mountain passes, putting miles on and returning to my little house.

I play with the cat. I read. I'm recovering from something I don't understand--a trauma, a wound I didn't know I had. I was too busy surviving.

One day I find an envelope from Landry in the bottom of my box at the post office. I wait until I get home to open it.

A glossy photo of him in uniform drops out. His face enraptures me all over again. He looks right at me with the green shading of his brown eyes. He stares straight ahead in military sternness but I remember the softness of his glance, the deep fullness of his gaze when we made love.

There's only the picture.

I trace his lips with my finger.

At the end of the month I join my ski-team friends and hike up the Mount Massive snow fields. Skiing down is a heady, exhilarating reward for the long climb with skis and poles slung over our shoulders.

We ride heaven.

I go to the Golden Burro and sit in my mother's station. She's cheerful and confused about why I left home but has made no effort to find me. She's aware people are watching so she's careful and smiles a lot.

We chat. I order. She has not heard from Rusty. Her legs bother her. Waitressing is hard on her feet. I can tell she's still drinking. I care but not really.

I love her but don't like her.

I see my father's Jeep in front of the Scarlet Inn Tavern with regularity but I don't go in.

I wait patiently for word from Rusty, my beautiful, quiet Navy brother.

Joel goes on missing.

Chapter 30

July is a beautiful month in the high Rockies. The daytime temperatures climb to seventy-five degrees and the nights hover at freezing. It's turning out to be a gorgeous summer with light afternoon clouds bringing short rains that turn the delicate green of the alpine meadows luxuriant.

I hear nothing in response to the flurry of head shots. Despite the glorious weather, there's a growing desperation in my soul.

Clyde, Steve and most of the Class of 1971 have gone into the mines. They are tired after work, establishing routines that will last them the rest of their lives.

I don't see them much.

They're adjusting to life in the cold and dark, working in grease-stained overalls and steel-toed boots. They're getting big paychecks.

They have rented houses in groups to sustain a party lifestyle, drinking beer and smoking pot. Black-light posters cover the walls and the scent of patchouli oil is in the air. Repetition is setting into their lives.

I stay home in the little house. Jethro and I spend hours cooking and cleaning and sitting on the porch, retiring for the night and curling up to dream.

Tina will be returning at the end of the month.

I need a plan and I don't have one.

Francie goes East to visit her family for two weeks and gives me the key to her house so I can check on things. I listen to the answering machine for both of us.

Colorado State University sends registration papers for classes and financial aid. They award me a full-ride scholarship with a few loans. I peruse the classes halfheartedly.

I walk in the woods among the aspen trees and the wildflowers in the high mountain sun. A fist inside me has begun to unclench. I'm no longer constantly angry.

I receive a letter from Landry. He says he's surviving the Marines. He tells me his thirteen weeks of boot camp will end in September.

Nothing more. I don't know what he means. He does not say he's coming home.

I refuse to think about it.

My dreams of him are vivid. I recall his intoxicating eyes and low voice.

I know Clyde feels caught in the middle. He's puzzled by the truce I've called.

I don't know any other way.

I'm afraid of sullying it. My memories are so heated. They are burned into my heart. I don't want to take the chance that Landry will tell me the sex was okay and what we had was good.

And nothing more.

I want to hold tightly to my belief that it was incredible, that it rocked the world and collapsed the stars. I refuse to let it be anything less than that.

"My choice," I declare.

I will take my heightened memories instead of Landry. I will choose my fantasy over a flat reality.

Chapter 31

August unfolds into Boom Days, the celebration of burro racing. I go down to watch the start of the race on Sunday morning but skip the rest of it.

I prefer to stay home. It's a privilege. I listen to music that is soft and gentle. I play Carole King's *Tapestry* endlessly.

I've found a quiet life for the first time. I savor every minute of it. I don't feel cold all the time anymore.

Sometimes I drive down to Mount Princeton Hot Springs and float in the pool, looking at the door to the room Landry and I shared for three days and three nights.

When I arrive at work, I unlock the rickety doors and climb the ancient stairs, lying on the bed where it all began.

I find myself pacing the stage and realize the call of the theater is boiling again in my blood.

One evening I stop the car in front of the house where Bette lives. I haven't seen her since the Food Town encounter.

My best friend has vanished into her marriage and her pregnancy. She has no phone so I couldn't call ahead. I drive around the block again.

There's a lamp in the window of the living room. Her husband's car is in the driveway. It's a ramshackle little house. It probably has four rooms.

I've never had any trouble with Danny but that was before they were married. I'm not sure how the marriage license has changed the dynamic.

I want to see her. I want to hear her sarcasm and snarky take on things.

I turn off the ignition, walk up and knock.

Danny opens the door and glares at me as if he doesn't recognize me.

"Hi, Danny," I venture.

"Oh. Hi, Maddie." He stands in the doorway and does not invite me in.

I hear Bette's voice from the kitchen. "Who is it, honey?"

"It's for you," he says.

Bette arrives from the kitchen, drying her hands on a dish towel.

"Look what the cat dragged in," she snipes warmly.

Danny steps aside but I catch the look that passes between them. He's warning her and she nods her acceptance of it.

She pulls me into a hug but blocks the door with her body.

Danny sits on the couch, opening a newspaper with a slap and pretending not to listen.

"Look at this shit," she says, pulling her shirt tight across her belly.

"Cool," I reply. "Does he kick?"

"Sure does, little whippersnapper," she says. "Like he's trying to break my ribs from the inside.

"Do you want to go for a drive?" I ask, knowing the answer before I ask.

"No, no. Damn, it would be fun but I'm in the middle of making biscuits. Maybe next week?" she says.

"Okay. Call me?"

"I go over to my mother's every day. I can call from there."

We both know she's not going to call.

"Can you believe I go to my mother's every day? Rose wins," she says.

The thought of Bette and Rose becoming close is incomprehensibly bizarre. It's a sign everything is changing, that everything has changed.

"I better get back to the kitchen," she snipes sarcastically. "Don't want to burn my goddamn biscuits."

"No," I say. "Don't want to burn them."

"Good luck at college."

"Thanks."

There's never been an opportunity to tell her about my head shots. Maybe it doesn't matter.

She does not ask about Landry.

She closes the door.

Chapter 32

I slink back to the car and drive away. I drive toward The Loop, allowing my creepy discomfort to give way to rage. I surrender to the anger. There's no reason not to. Anger empowers me. It always has.

I fly down the straightaway toward the curves where I can float on smoking tires. I feel a screaming need to turn around and snatch Bette from the clutches of the demon behind the newspaper. I want to seize her from the world of sexual power and politics, the intricate dance that obviously sustains a marriage.

It's not the first time I've seen it. I've watched it my entire life, peering through the bars of my crib-
-my mother's submission and coyness in the face of my father's assumption of power.

The ugly dance always sharpens when alcohol comes into it. Booze is the element that reduces the game to base levels, to the lowest tier of human behavior.

I drop a gear in the Camaro, sending the back tires into a smoky, growly spin. I love the heady feeling of the drop and the lift that comes as I play the clutch.

I hear myself purring like a cat. I steer through the three turns like I'm possessed. The car polishes the blacktop, caressing its surface with smoke and tire marks.

When I rocket out the other end, I slam the Led Zeppelin tape into the 8 track and let Jimmy Page take it from there. I'm doing 140 when I pass the Seppi homestead.

"Feeling better now, Cupcake?" I imagine Bette's sarcastic question from the seat beside me. I can hear the snarky tone that always makes me laugh.

I answer her out loud, "As a matter of fact…"

I hear her laugh ring like a bell in the car, joining the Led Zeppelin track.

"I can't quit you, babe, so I'm gonna put you down for a while," sings Robert Plant in full blues mode.

It will have to do.

Returning to town, I unlock the door to Francie's house She will be home tomorrow. The message light flashes on the machine and I press the play button.

"Francie, this is Charlie Marshall," the man's voice says.

Charlie is an assistant professor of communications at Colorado Mountain College. I've done community theater with him since his arrival three years ago. He's not especially warm or charming but he gets the job done and he directs strong, solid stage productions.

"I've been trying to get in touch with Maddie," he says.

I jump at the sound of my name.

"I got the grant to film *Trails* and I want her to play Annie again."

Trails. A great piece of theater on a minimalist stage. It's a play about choices and how every choice affects everything thereafter. It's a four-actor production and I love my part—Annie.

I transform from Annie as a child to a junkie to a dowdy matron. The parts are all written that way—every actor's dream—to play multiple personalities ranging from ages six to sixty.

This is the answer to the boiling in my blood.

"Anyway, if you can get in touch with her, tell her to give me a call. As soon as possible. 486-5555. Thanks. Hope you're doing well."

The answering machine clicks off and I reach for the phone.

Did he say film? I think to myself.

Charlie answers on the second ring. I try not to sound exuberant but I can't conceal it. He's used to my enthusiasm.

"Charlie, it's Maddie. Just got your message. Hope it's not too late. I would LOVE to do *Trails* again!"

"Great, Maddie. I'm glad you're available. I've been in touch with the rest of the cast. Everyone's still in town. Do you have the script?" he asks.

"I'm sure of it."

"I need to make some changes to go to film but that will be easy. It's such an austere and adaptable piece. Can you come to a table read tomorrow?"

"Of course!" I'm so ready for this.

When we hang up, I realize that he did.

He said, "Film."

Chapter 33

Trails. I pull out the script when I get home. I remember the lines. I'm wired, wandering the house reciting the words to the cat. He's an appreciative audience but only because I have treats in my pocket.

"I'm not gonna play with you, Georgie. You're mean," I tell the cat.

It's great fun to age so dramatically in a piece of theater. At six-years-old, the voices and language are innocent but also reflective of family influence and cultural norms. There's already savagery among the young children, as in real life.

The play is for adolescents and asks tough questions of its audience about what life dishes out. The scenes loop and arc back on themselves architecturally.

"No wonder Charlie got a grant for this," I tell Jethro, remembering how good the play is.

"I shall reprise my stage role for the film," I announce in haughty accent.

Jethro is silent.

When I fall asleep, dreams of the play push out the dreams of Landry. I hear the lines in my head. I recall the applause after performances.

I can't wait to see my fellow actors again—Wally, who graduated last year and is recovering from an accident in the mine; Johnny, who is a year behind me in school and loves singing more than anything; and Allison, who is a great skier and might qualify for Junior Nationals this year. I've seen each of them in passing this summer, with no time to sit down and talk.

I wake easily, singing to Jethro and the morning, serenading my bowl of Cheerios, before running off to work, floating through my tours of the day.

At lunchtime, the Three N's and I sit on the stage and eat sandwiches and chips. They regale me with stories about their adventures in romance, their troubles at home and the latest movies.

Nan proclaims the emotionality of *Love Story*. Nora votes for the hilarity of *Bananas*. Nancy swoons over *Summer of '42* and I concur, making it Best Movie of the Year as awarded by the staff of the Tabor Opera House.

After work I whip up a salad, reciting lines in my head as I move about the kitchen, Jethro in close attendance.

Throwing on a sweater, I drive up the hill to the college. I took classes at the college during high school and performed in plays there so I know my way around. In any case it's only two buildings-- hard to get lost.

When I reach the communications lab, Charlie is setting up, efficient and no-nonsense as ever.

"Maddie!" says Charlie, glancing up. "Grab a couple of chairs, will you?"

I carry the chairs to the table and see the pile of scripts. My fingers tingle to touch them.

Johnny arrives next, whistling his way into the lab, happy to be part of the adventure.

Allison and Wally walk in together. Allison is inspecting the scars along Wally's jaw.

"Crusher caught my sleeve," explains Wally. "Pulled my arm in before I knew what was happening. Swallowed me to the shoulder and then my head hung up on the gears. Kept slamming my jaw until they got it shut down. Broke it sixteen times."

I wander over out of curiosity to see the holes where the external fixators held the lower part of his face on while the bones healed.

"Three months of applesauce and pureed potatoes," he laughs. "They wired my teeth together so I couldn't open my mouth. Tell you one thing—don't get sick when your jaws are wired shut."

I watch Allison wrinkle up her face and I have to hold myself back from doing the same.

Charlie gets our attention and walks us through the new studio. He shows us the lighting and sound equipment purchased with the money from the grant, along with the new camera, an Aeroflex 16mm. Sound will be a Sennheiser overhead microphone attached to a Nagra recorder made in Switzerland--a reel-to-reel tape machine with sync sound.

Charlie motions to the editing table. "I know flatbed editors are coming into vogue," he tells us. "But I can get by with this Moviola just fine." The machine stands imposing and upright. The dials, switches and viewing box, complete with multiple reels, look intimating.

The four of us are neophytes to film. The equipment fascinates me.

So this is how the magic is made, I think.

My toes dance in my shoes.

I want to be in front of that camera. But I also want to be behind the camera. I want to do it all-- hold the microphone in the air over a developing scene, work the sync machine to match the sound to the action, play with the Moviola to see what I can do with pacing and depth.

I feel like I've been shot from a cannon. This is what lights me up. This is what boils the blood in my veins.

We sit at the table and go over our schedules. The toughest scenes to coordinate will be the four of us together. Except for Wally, we're all working. We get it figured out utilizing weekends and evenings. The format of the script calls for many individual scenes and, because of that, we can shoot it in two weeks.

"I want to run the camera. I want to work sound. I want to edit," I hear myself say out loud.

Charlie's eyebrows jump.

Maybe I sound like a lunatic but I mean every word of it.

"Fine, fine," he says. "Great."

I'm not surprised that he accepts this as my norm because it is. I want it all.

Charlie hands out the revised copies of the script.

"I started to make changes but then I looked at the bones of it," Charlie says. "It's sparse. It's supposed to be sparse. So we're shooting all the action shots here in the studio. I'll film some pick-up shots outside to colorize the film but your scenes will be controlled. Nothing outside. No locations. No background noise to contend with. With this shoot schedule, that's the only way it will work. We can use more costumes and makeup but for the most part, I've left the script alone. It's effective the way it is."

We listen closely.

"You're comfortable on stage," Charlie continues. "When you get in front of a camera, there's a big difference. On stage, you project your emotions. On camera, you feel your emotions. The camera picks up every twitch. Everything is subtle."

It feels like old times. I close my eyes and a shudder runs through me. I can feel my blood flatten out and start to bubble. Goosebumps pop out on my arms.

We pick up the scripts. Johnny speaks the first line, "Vroom, vroom, beep, beep."

And I cry, "Georgie, you mashed my castle!"

Chapter 34

With *Trails*, my life bounces. Filming starts immediately. We play with the camera the first night. Charlie shoots us under lights so we can see the differences he's talking about.

The exaggerated motions and expressions used on stage look phony and ridiculous on film. The camera picks up the slightest movement and amplifies it. The acting must be nuanced and subtle, felt instead of projected because the camera is invasively close. There's no distance to the audience. In close-up, the actor is inches away.

When we accidentally glance at the camera, it plays back as a jarring disruption of boundary.

"Don't look at the camera. Don't look at the camera," we remind ourselves on an endless loop.

We will get used to it but when the camera is a foot from our noses, it's disconcerting.

"Forget the camera. Don't let that awareness register in your eyes," coaches Charlie.

We learn the trick of focus. It avoids the distracted look when our peripheral vision is conscious of the camera.

Within hours I learn an immense respect for screen actors and their ability to ignore the camera and focus on a non-existent spot in mid-air. It's a skill requiring acute concentration.

"This is exhausting," I declare at midnight, collapsing on the carpet.

My fellow actors agree, heaving themselves into chairs.

We wrap up for the night. I fall into bed weary to the bone from the effort at narrowing my focus.

I dream of Landry. My body confirms it in the morning when I wake in luxurious yearning for him. But I'm too tired to remember the dreams and that's a good thing. It prevents me from writing the embarrassing letter tingling at my fingertips every time I pick up a pen.

During the day, Charlie films pick-up shots to add color to the film. I rush to the college as soon as I lock up the Opera House. We rehearse scenes out of order, the way movies are shot.

I'm on fire.

We learn how frustrating and disturbing it is to jump into a scene without the emotional build-up that occurs on stage. Theater productions run from beginning to end, through all the emotive highs and lows. On stage the actors are carried on the tide of the play, responding to the energy of the scene and the audience.

"With film, there's no audience, no continuity and usually nobody with you in front of the camera," explains Charlie.

We experiment with preparation techniques-- wandering the halls muttering lines, hunkering down in a corner and concentrating on building emotionality, distracting ourselves until the last second and then snapping our attention to the scene.

"Explains a lot about screen actors, doesn't it?" observes Charlie, the exercise confirming why screen actors seem so much more unstable than stage actors.

The demands for temperamental volatility in film are crazy-making. We wobble through the night attempting to synthesize this new world.

"Cry!" demands Charlie and we look at him dumbfounded and dry-eyed.

We've got a ways to go.

Chapter 35

I stand in the Post Office ripping open a letter from Rusty.

"Hi, baby girl!" he starts and I watch the handwriting on the page get blurry.

I brush away the tears and read on.

"I wrote you that we were in the Mediterranean but it wasn't true. I didn't want you to worry. For your graduation, the Kitty Hawk was in Vietnam for our 6th Line Period in 7 months. We were at Yankee Station and it was tough."

For Rusty to say something is tough, it must have been horrendous.

"But here's your late Graduation present: I'm in San Diego. We left Vietnam on June 23, got to the Philippines on June 26, Hawaii on July 11 and San Diego on July 17."

He's on the mainland! He's safe! I catch myself standing on my toes as I continue reading.

"I spent a few days celebrating with my shipmates and planned to show up and surprise you. But then Maria happened."

Maria?

"I met her in a restaurant one night. She's from Mexico but speaks English. She's been here for five years. I've met her family and they're all great cooks. Love the tortillas!"

I can hear him laughing.

"I'm learning Spanish. Can you picture it?"

He writes that Maria is beautiful, with dark, curly hair and soft green eyes. She's studying nursing and cleans rooms to make money. She's the oldest and he has fun kidding her little brothers.

"The boys are named Juan and Robert. We play soccer in the back yard."

I can tell he's falling in love with Maria. He's such a softy, his quiet heart broken often in high school by the callous games teenage girls play.

"I got your pictures and have mixed feelings about you not going to college. You know I've got your back no matter what you decide. You'll be a success whatever path you take."

I feel my throat tighten.

"I'm glad you're out of the house. Tina's place sounds wonderful. I laughed at the stories about the cat. I can't picture you with a cat but I guess it's good."

He's been getting my letters.

"Thanks for all the news and gossip. Sorry to hear about Henry. I don't suppose there's anything on Joel?"

I know Rusty thinks about Joel every day, like I do. Joel was a natural athlete, always throwing a ball. When we walked anywhere, he threw a ball in the air. Catch and throw. Catch and throw.

I was the little sister. Joel was the oldest brother. He was vivacious and funny, his red hair always curly and unkempt on his head. He was tall and strong and all the girls were crazy about him. He could ski like the wind.

We have run through the possibilities so often in our heads--a stroke or heart attack felling him; a kidnapping that will resolve in his knocking on my door someday; a running away from all of the craziness of home--a scenario in which I fantasize about finding him some day in Juneau, Alaska, happily married with six small children.

And of course, the worst of the worst–tortured and murdered and buried in someone's basement. It runs in my head like a hamster on a wheel, constantly squeaking in my brain.

It's a horror.

If I walk around the corner, will he be there? When I wake in the morning, will I hear his laugh in the kitchen? If I check the mail regularly, will there someday be a letter?

In all the time I've tried to hook onto him, communicate with him, I've never felt a connection. But I've never felt an absence of him either. It could drive one mad--the not knowing.

Chapter 36

I carry Rusty's letter with me everywhere. I don't know when I'll see him but it will be soon, I'm sure of it. He's alive and he's mainland. The Kitty Hawk has gone into cold iron for a thirty-day stand-down and the crew is on leave and liberty.

I smile all the time. I am rampantly happy because of Rusty and the film. I think about them day and night.

I run to help Charlie every chance I get--setting up shots, running errands, working the light meter and microphones. I'm picking it up as fast as I can.

I cheerfully lead tours at the Opera House during the day. I supervise the Three N's and we enjoy meeting people from Oklahoma, New York, California, Florida, Toronto, Mexico City.

I've taught the girls to have fun with the job, making bearable the repetition of it. We laugh along with the crazy comments made by people who have no clue of the ferocity of life in a small, isolated town at 10,000 feet.

In the mornings I have strange dreams about Joel--he's twelve years old, climbing a pine tree by the cemetery, standing on a branch and laughing down at me.

I wake and the dreams unsettle me.

Jethro stands in the kitchen window as I wash the remnants of Cheerios from a bowl. I talk to him and he answers me. He talks back now.

We have the perfect living arrangement. I wish it could go on indefinitely but when Tina returns, it will be time for me to move on.

The drifty, rootless feeling of my life takes its toll. I appreciate having a roof over my head, the quiet intimacy of a home. But I know it can't last. I will cherish it and let go when it's time to roam.

One magnificent August day I take the Camaro out for lunch, eating a sandwich as I drive around Turquoise Lake. A few airless clouds reflect in the water of the lake. I see an eagle's nest at the top of a tall pine.

I drive too fast, shifting down and sliding through curves when visibility is unimpaired. I play Cream at top volume, my windows down, breathing the glorious Colorado wind that blows through my windows.

"Silver horses run down moonbeams in your dark eyes," croons Jack Bruce.

At 5:00 I lock the doors of the Opera House, pointing the Camaro to the college. We're filming my favorite scene. I shoot heroin tonight. I can't wait to see it on film.

I drop my bag on the floor as I enter the studio.

"Hi!" I call out.

Charlie is bustling around and there's a stranger with him. He's Charlie's age but unlike Charlie, who is short and balding, the man, also in his forties, is tall and thin with an elegant, pointed nose. The stranger looks at me with interest.

Charlie looks up. "Hey, Maddie. You have fifteen minutes to get ready. This is Foster Lane, an old friend of mine from college."

"Hello, Mr. Lane," I say, approaching to shake his hand.

"Call me Foster"

"Foster."

We shake hands and he looks closely in my eyes. He doesn't scare me but I register his scrutiny and wonder if he does this with everyone. His look is penetrating.

"Foster's passing through from California. We're catching up on old times. He's going to sit in tonight."

"Terrific! Charlie is a pro," I tell Foster.

"Maybe I can learn a thing or two," he says, winking at Charlie. "We reconnect every year or two. End up laughing all night, drinking too much and completely losing track of time and obligations."

"Cool," I say. "It's great to meet you. If you'll excuse me, I need to change."

I think about Foster Lane as I apply makeup and pull on my costume. I wonder what he'll think of the magic we're about to slap down on celluloid.

When I return, the college crew is there. Three students are back on campus early to work on the film. I like them. They're spacey and self-important but I find it endearing.

We laugh at each other's jokes and the atmosphere is easy and cordial.

Charlie demonstrates my position in front of the camera. We discuss the physical parameters of the framing. He calls the crew into position and Foster volunteers to clap the sound board.

Charlie gives me a moment to find the door to my character, a bitter junkie who reeks of tragedy and lost promise.

He calls, "Action."

I wrap the strap and tighten it around my arm. Charlie and I have rehearsed the camera's angle on the needle so it looks real. I wait, allowing the sensation to flow through my veins.

"Yeah," I say heavily.

My eyes roll back in my head and I let everything slow down.

"Yeah, baby," I intone.

I fumble with the strap and lazily free it.

"Give it," I say, slipping into the nod. I let my head drop twice and open my eyes to confront the camera.

"So," I say with challenge and bite in my voice. My eyes close and I fight to reopen them. I slur my words.

"So what?" I ask. "You think you're so much better. Name of the game's sedation. Right? Whole world's looking for a way out."

I feel the scene tingling under my skin. I take my time.

When I say the last line, "Big deal," I slip into drug oblivion.

Charlie lets the camera run. The only sound I hear is my breathing and the whir of the camera.

When Charlie finally says, "Cut," I keep my eyes closed and let the character drain out of me.

I hear Charlie say something and see Foster standing at his shoulder, looking into the camera playback with Charlie.

What Charlie said is, "See what I mean?"

Foster watches the playback thoughtfully. He does not say anything for a long time.

Very quietly, he says, "Yeah, I see it."

Chapter 37

We are fully charged and film *Trails* at breakneck speed. Every free moment, we're in front of the camera or behind the camera or holding a microphone or reflecting light into someone's face.

And then we're done. Charlie calls it and we wrap, dropping directly into editing.

We work with the 16mm film, a delicate but forgiving format, syncing sound and cutting and taping at the Moviola. We hunch over the machine long into the night, sometimes with the full college crew, sometimes only Charlie and me.

He asks me about my plans and, in the darkness of the editing room, I tell him about the head shots and the dreams I mailed out with them.

He nods his head.

I'm not sure what his reticence means. I tell him about the vast silence I got in response to my dispatches.

"My roommate assignment at CSU is a cowgirl from Brush," I say woefully.

He laughs.

He asks me questions and listens hard to my answers. He asks me the same things three or four times, in different ways—like he's testing me.

He stops to show me a trick, a technique, for editing. And he goes back to questioning me.

I see Francie when she gets home from her trip. She wants to see *Trails* on screen, the finished product. But there's something else, too.

She and Charlie are talking and they're talking a lot. I want to believe they're discussing future projects for community theater but I have a gnawing sense they're talking about me.

Summer winds down. I hear nothing from Bette. Our lunch does not materialize and I find myself turning her into an imaginary friend.

"I think they're talking about me," I say to the invisible Bette over dinner one night.

"And why would you think that?" she asks, her light sarcasm putting things into perspective for me.

"I'm not sure," I say. "I must be going crazy."

"I could have told you that in junior high," she quips. "Should I smack you upside the head?"

"No, I think I'll be okay," I laugh at my ability to imagine exactly how this conversation would go. "I'll just be trundling along."

"You do that," she says.

I haven't had time for Clyde or Steve and they haven't had time for me. Their lives are filled up with shift work at Climax and partying.

Steve tells me that Henry's father has taken to motoring around Twin Lakes in a boat he purchased for the purpose. He drinks too much on the boat. The assistance of friends has dropped off so he's often out there drunk and alone.

Henry's mother busies herself with church and promoting the idea of grandchildren to her daughters. She sews baby blankets in hope.

My conversations with Steve drop off into long silences. He invites me to parties but I don't go. I do the same thing to Clyde.

I can feel the distance developing even as I refuse to acknowledge it. I want us to be close for the rest of our lives. I want us to live up to the potential I've always seen in us.

These are my friends from childhood. I cannot fathom life without them but we're drifting apart. We're riding different currents and we're getting farther away from each other.

It's the same with Bette. I've managed to turn a real person into an imaginary friend. She might as well be on another planet. I might as well be on another planet.

They're doing what people do. I'm the one who is making a film and dreaming of Hollywood.

How much more out of touch can I get?

Chapter 38

Everything I own is back in garbage bags. Tina arrives tomorrow. I've replaced her spices, teas and condiments.

My heart drops when I think about loading my belongings into the Camaro and heading to Fort Collins, accepting the scholarship and moving into a room with the rodeo queen from Brush.

I eat a last lunch with the Three N's. The girls giggle in anticipation of school starting. Their faces are enchanting and guileless.

I'll leave without saying goodbye to either my mother or father. Rusty encourages me to visit them, or at least to call, but he of all people understands why I have no interest.

Their betrayal runs so deep they lost their hold on us long ago.

I'll send them a postcard from college with my forwarding address. The only reason to stay in touch is Joel. We will wait for the knock on the door, the phone call, the letter in the mail. We'll always be holding our breath. It's all we have in common.

Rusty is on the mainland and I'll see him soon. I'll meet Maria and her little brothers and watch a soccer game in her parents' backyard.

I cherish my memories of Landry. He has changed everything for me, introducing me to the world of intimacy. My body's response to him was like rocketing to the moon. I've only begun to experience my sexuality but I know it will be an amazing journey, a pathway to the stars.

Charlie sits alone in the dark editing room when I arrive. I'm a few minutes late because I've been flying through curves in the Camaro, smoking the tires and spraying fire to settle the screeching in my head.

Just like Rusty taught me.

"Sit down, Maddie." Charlie's tone is grave. "Do you know who Foster Lane is?"

"Your friend from college?" I ask tentatively.

"Right, my friend from college."

"Okay," I say hesitantly.

"We were theater majors. After college, we went to L.A. together, to make our way in the movie business."

I don't understand where he's going with this.

"I couldn't find my place out there. I buckled and went to graduate school and began teaching."

"Okay," I repeat.

"Foster Lane didn't buckle. Maybe he had more talent. Maybe he had more luck. Whatever it was, he made it. He's the real deal."

A chill rushes up my spine.

"He's a film director. He makes big movies. I didn't make it. But he did."

I sit waiting for whatever's coming next.

"He wants to talk to you," he says, reaching for the phone. He dials. Foster answers.

"Foster, this is Charlie. She's here. I'm handing you over," he says.

He hands me the receiver and I put it to my ear.

"Foster?"

"Maddie, I don't know how much Charlie has told you about my new film. I'm impressed with you-- the way you look on camera, your range for being so young. I have a small part for you in this movie if you want it."

All the air sucks out of the room. Here it is--the door swinging open.

I say one word and there's no hesitation.

"Yes."

The End

TRAILS

A Stage Play by Carol Bellhouse

Copyright 2013 Carol Bellhouse

Feel free to perform this play without charge.
Let me know how it goes.
CarolBellhouse@gmail.com

TRAILS
by Carol Bellhouse

The stage has two areas of action. In one area, there is a stool and a coat rack on which hang a military pilot's cap, white jacket, ratty cardigan sweater, tiara and clerical collar. In the other area is a sandbox. The sand and toys are imaginary but four children play intently and gleefully in the sandbox, pouring sand from buckets, making truck noises, and maneuvering their cars over roadways.

The children are six years old but played by adult actors: Randall is tall and handsome with blonde hair and blue eyes. Sophia is short and bouncy with dark hair and eyes. Anne is a tall, gorgeous blonde with blue eyes and a statuesque body. George has brown hair and eyes, with a small frame and chiseled features.

GEORGE
Vroom. Vroom. Bee-beep!

ANNE
Georgie! You mashed my castle!

GEORGE
It is in the way!

ANNE
I'm not gonna play with you, Georgie. You're mean.

She rubs her eyes tearfully.

RANDALL
We can build it even better, Annie.

Randall begins rebuilding the sandcastle.
Anne sobs and Sophia pats her on the
shoulder.

SOPHIA
Don't cry, Annie.

RANDALL
See, there's the door.

SOPHIA
Randy is building it good.

George sneers.

ANNE
Will you marry me someday, Randy?

Randall shakes his head no but is kind.

RANDALL
No, I have to go fly jets.

Randall picks up an imaginary plane and
begins strafing a corner of the sandbox.

RANDALL (CONT'D)
(in military voice)
We have the target in sight, Captain.
Fire when ready. Rat a tat a tat.

Anne looks up at him in admiration.

ANNE

Gee, Randy. You really gonna be a pilot?

RANDALL
Darn right I am! I'm not gonna spend my whole life at the playground. I'm gonna see the world!

SOPHIA
I'm gonna stay home with my mom and my cat.

GEORGE
You can't. You have to BE something when you grow up.

SOPHIA
No, I don't.

GEORGE
Yes, you do.

SOPHIA
No, I don't.

GEORGE
Yes, you do.

SOPHIA
(exasperated)
Alright, smarty-pants. What are YOU gonna be?

GEORGE
Preacher. Like my dad.

MOTHER'S VOICE

Randy! Randy! Lunch is ready!

RANDALL
Coming, Mommy!

Randall jumps up and brushes the sand off his pants. Anne blows him a kiss but Randall doesn't notice. He runs toward the stool area, making jet noises and flying his plane through the air, and as he reaches the stool, he becomes an adult.

GEORGE
He can't be a pilot.

SOPHIA
Can too!

GEORGE
Can not!

SOPHIA
Can too!

ANNE
Yeah!

SOPHIA
Randy can be anything he wants.

ANNE
Yeah!

SOPHIA
There's lots of things he can be.

ANNE

Yeah! Even a pilot.

Randall sits on the stool. The children in the sandbox continue playing, as they do though each monologue. Their play is silent.

> RANDALL
> (to the audience)
> Playing in the sandbox, all we had were possibilities...so many possibilities. Every moment is a crossroads. Any instant can make the difference. Will I really fly jets? Or will I repair lawnmowers, settling down young and marrying my high school sweetheart...
> (he nods toward Anne)
> Who will just happen to be Annie.

He smiles at the irony of it.

> RANDALL (CONT'D)
> Half a step at the crossroads could lead me to prison. So easy to take that first car. Who knows what my choices will be and what I will make of them? If you drop a leaf in a stream, everything affects its course—the shape of the leaf, a random rock, a sudden breeze. So many different paths. For me.

He nods to each child in the sandbox as he says his or her name.

                    RANDALL (CONT'D)
          For Annie. Sophie. Georgie. You.

Randall gets up and moves down into the
audience, questioning a man directly.

                    RANDALL (CONT'D)
          How different would YOUR life be—if
          YOU'D gotten your degree?

He looks at another man.

                    RANDALL (CONT'D)
          Or if YOU hadn't.

He asks of a woman--

                    RANDALL (CONT'D)
          If YOU'D moved to New York City?

He asks of another woman--

                    RANDALL (CONT'D)
          Or YOU'D never left home?

He questions a man--

                    RANDALL (CONT'D)
          What if YOU'D married your high
          school sweetheart?

He turns his attention to a woman--

                    RANDALL (CONT'D)
          What if YOU hadn't?

Randall moves back toward the stage. As an afterthought, he stops to ask one more quiet question of a man in the audience.

>   RANDALL (CONT'D)
>   What if the person YOU loved most
>   put a bullet through her head?

He returns to the stage and turns back to the audience.

>   RANDALL (CONT'D)
>   Crossroads. Totally different lives just
>   half a step apart. If I became a jet
>   pilot...

Randall lifts the pilot's cap off the coat rack and places it carefully and professionally on his head. As he does so, he ages 25 years. His expression becomes stern and weary. He moves stiffly from his war wounds and specifically, the back injury. His voice changes and becomes military.

>   RANDALL (CONT'D)
>   Looking back, I made all the right
>   choices.

He says it as if to convince himself as much as the audience.

>   RANDALL (CONT'D)

Graduated from high school. Captain of the ski team. Good grades. President of the senior class. Recommended to the Air Force Academy in Colorado Springs. The Academy was excellent training. Made a man of me. Proudest moment of my life was getting my wings. Became a flight commander and was shot down over Mashhad. Won a Purple Heart and became a flight instructor.

Randall sits uncomfortably, weary from his old injuries. He flinches in pain when he moves.

RANDALL (CONT'D)
Won medals, commendations. Not bad for a small-town boy.

He pauses as if listening to a question from the audience. He smiles ironically before he answers.

RANDALL (CONT'D)
Disappointments?

He shrugs, uncomfortable with the personal nature of the question.

RANDALL (CONT'D)
There have been, certainly. Divorced. For the third time. No children. Somehow time just got away from me.

He listens to another silent, personal question, again uncomfortable.

                    RANDALL (CONT'D)
     Alone?

He thinks. Obviously, he is a man in total isolation, holding tightly to his sense of honor.

                    RANDALL (CONT'D)
          Never thought of it that way. Did my
          duty for God and country. Did what
          had to be done. Proud of my
          contribution. Mighty proud.

In the sandbox, Anne exultantly throws up her arms.

                    ANNE
          I'm gonna be a doctor and take care
          of people and dogs.

The children resume playing aloud. Randall sits perfectly still for a moment. Then he slowly removes his hat and hangs it on the rack. He gets up and walks stiffly back toward the sandbox.

                    GEORGE
                    (fighting)
          Fat chance, Annie.

                    ANNE
                    (screaming)

I am too! And you can't stop me.
You're a brat!

George sticks out his tongue at her.

                    GEORGE
Nyah nyah!

                    ANNE
                    (in a rage, she throws
                    an imaginary shovel)
I hate you, Georgie!

Anne jumps up and stomps her feet.

                ANNE (CONT'D)
I hate you! I hate you! I hate you!

Anne jumps out of the sandbox, wailing in
fury. She runs toward the stool, slowing as
she reaches it and becomes an adult. As
Anne and Randall pass each other, they do
not make eye contact.

                    SOPHIA
You are so rotten, Georgie.

                    GEORGE
Nyah.

Sophia glares at him.

George glares back for a moment, then
drops his eyes. He feebly gets in the last
word.

                GEORGE (CONT'D)

(under his breath)
Nyah.

When Anne reaches the stool, her expression is glowing peacefulness. Now matronly, she puts on the white coat and pats it.

ANNE
(to the audience)
My life...

She looks at the audience and then she smiles her sweetest grandmotherly smile and plays her joke on the audience.

ANNE (CONT'D)
No, I'm not a doctor. I didn't finish medical school. Don't remember starting even. Never made it to college, come to think of it.

She giggles sweetly.

ANNE (CONT'D)
In fact...

She wrinkles up her nose and grins.

ANNE (CONT'D)
I never finished high school!

She seats her extra pounds with some difficulty on the stool.

ANNE (CONT'D)

Actually, I work in the pet department at J.C. Penny's. We have the cutest puppy! You should see him. He barks so hard, it knocks him down! He's a love. Let me show you pictures of my six beautiful children. I'm a grandma eight times over.

She reaches in her pocket.

ANNE (CONT'D)
Oops! I forgot my picture book, you know those little folders…

She waves off her oversight and giggles.

ANNE (CONT'D)
I married a farmer. I'm a farmer's wife. We live on the plains of Eastern Colorado. And I can't imagine being happier. We keep a hundred and forty head of dairy cows. Whoever would have thought?

She muses.

ANNE (CONT'D)
In high school, I was a cheerleader, homecoming queen, prom queen… And now my greatest joy is singing a duet with my daughter in church on Sunday. I know I've gained some weight. That's because--

She winks at the audience.

ANNE (CONT'D)

I make the best chocolate cake in four counties. Life's been very, very good to me. Oh, there's been hard times, sure. My parents both died when I was fourteen. One of my sons is paralyzed from the neck down. Diving accident. You never know what life's going to hand you. But life's a gift and each new day's like opening a Christmas present.

She nods to make her point. Then she checks her imaginary watch.

ANNE (CONT'D)
Well, my break's over. Time to clean more cages. Stop by again sometime. I mean that.

Randall, who has been standing by the sandbox, suddenly becomes a child again and flies his imaginary plane with sound effects as he jumps into the play area. He stops and looks at Sophia and George, who are playing silently and angrily, their backs to each other.

RANDALL
Where's Annie?

SOPHIA
She ran away. Georgie made her mad.

Anne stands and takes off the coat. George looks down sheepishly. Anne hangs up the coat.

RANDALL
Where did she go?

He looks around and sees her standing by the stool. Randall calls to her.

RANDALL (CONT'D)
Annie! Annie!

Anne, now six-years-old again, looks at him with a stubborn little-girl pout.

Randall waves for her to come back.

RANDALL (CONT'D)
Come back, Annie.

Sophia joins in the plea.

SOPHIA
Please, Annie!

Anne capitulates and smiles, skipping from the stool to the sandbox. She stops and glares at George, her hands on her hips.

ANNE
I'll only come back if you promise to be nice.

George smirks at her.

Randall catches his eye and gives him a menacing look.

                    RANDALL
        Georgie…

George shrugs.

                    GEORGE
        Oh, all right.

Anne smiles in triumph and settles into the sandbox.

                    GEORGE (CONT'D)
                    (faking a smile)
        I promise to be good.

                    ANNE
        Okay.

George sneers and destroys her castle again.

                    GEORGE
        I lied!

Anne shrieks and bursts into tears.

Sophia yells at him.

                    SOPHIA
        Georgie!

Angrily, Randall pushes George, who falls out of the sandbox.

GEORGE
Ow, ow, ow, Mommy, Mommy!

Randall cuddles Anne's head against his chest as she wails loudly.

Sophia strokes Anne's hair helplessly.

George runs crying toward the stool, aging to an adult as he sits on it.

SOPHIA
Don't cry, Annie. He's a dumb-head.

RANDALL
We'll build it again. Even better.

Anne brushes the tears from her eyes.

ANNE
We will?

RANDALL
Sure!

Anne stares up at Randall with glistening eyes.

ANNE
Will you marry me, Randy?

Randall shakes his head, smiles and resumes playing silently.

George has put on the moth-eaten cardigan sweater. He sits twitching on the stool. He manically grabs at the back of his neck.

                    GEORGE
You want to know what happens to
me?

He grabs his neck again, his eyes jittering
across the audience, unable to make
contact with anyone.

                GEORGE (CONT'D)
What?

He is hearing voices.

                GEORGE (CONT'D)
I have the biggest import business in
the United States. Travel to a lot of
exotic countries. China and Russia
last week. Remind me to show you
some slides before you leave.

He jumps up from the stool and moves in
jerks around the stage. He grabs his neck
again.

                GEORGE (CONT'D)
Didn't go to college. I'm a self-made
man. School of life, as they say. Just
got out there and showed them what I
could do.

He looks up at the ceiling.

                GEORGE (CONT'D)

What? My daffodils look lovely, don't they? I never got married. Had plenty of offers. The most beautiful women in the world. A Thai princess…Italian heiress…you name it, I've had them all. But I could never find one quite good enough…one with ALL the qualities I wanted. Remind me to show you some slides before you leave.

George never left home. He was diagnosed with schizophrenia long ago and lives in a fantasy world. He is confused and lacks coherence when he talks.

GEORGE (CONT'D)
I went to Harvard, of course. Twenty-five year reunion this summer. Graduated with highest honors. Opened a lot of doors for me, let me tell you. What?

He sits on the stool but continues to fidget nervously.

GEORGE (CONT'D)
Have you ever thought about linoleum? Who invented that word? I want a sextant for Christmas. Remind me to show you some slides before you leave…

He squirms uncomfortably on the stool and finally jumps up, unable to stay still. His eyes dart around the audience as he grabs his neck again.

                    GEORGE (CONT'D)
          What? Have I told you what business
          I'm in? Real estate. Florida. Miami,
          mostly. Off-shore oil ventures. Bearer
          bonds.

George sits down and starts nodding his head, pleading with the audience to believe him.

                    GEORGE (CONT'D)
          My ultimate goal in life is to produce
          self-help tapes. Build people's self-
          confidence and teach them how to
          succeed. Like me

                    MOTHER'S VOICE
          Georgie? Georgie! It's time for my
          medicine.

The quavery voice calls from offstage. George continues to nod his head at the audience.

                    GEORGE
          My mother. She's an invalid.

He calls out to her.

                    GEORGE (CONT'D)
          Coming, Mother.

He turns back to the audience.

GEORGE (CONT'D)
You must excuse me now. I'm expecting an important call from the Pentagon. I'm a defense contractor, you see. Very important.

In the sandbox, Sophia jumps up in triumph.

SOPHIA
There! Good as new!

They have rebuilt Anne's sandcastle. George removes his sweater and hangs it on the coat rack.

Anne smiles her thanks sweetly to Sophia and Randall. George slips on a clerical collar.

SOPHIA (CONT'D)
I hope Georgie gets hit by a car. It would knock some sense into him.

Anne looks at her innocently. In a loud, earnest voice, she asks,

ANNE
It would?

George sits on the stool in his clerical collar. His face is worn from care. He does not move his legs. They dangle uselessly off the stool. His tone is soft and gentle.

GEORGE

Ah, the twists and turns of life. You aim in one direction and life sends you in another. Who knows what Providence has in store? It calls to mind the Robert Frost poem of two roads diverging in the wood. "And I...I took the road less traveled by...And that has made all the difference." After high school, my road took me to state college.

With an incredulous, resigned humor, he announces:

GEORGE (CONT'D)
Sophomore year I was hit by a car. As you can see.

He motions to his lifeless legs.

GEORGE (CONT'D)
I can still walk with a cane and these horrid braces. Lucky to be alive. Praise God for that. The accident was the turning point in my life. In the hospital, I rethought my hopes, my dreams, my goals. And went into the ministry. Preacher like my father, whoever would have thought? It's been arduous and fulfilling. Tedious and challenging. My wife and I had two children. One died of spina bifida and the other is lost to us. We don't know where she is. She ran away many years ago.

He shakes his head sadly. Almost as a benediction, he says:

> GEORGE (CONT'D)
> There are joys and there are sorrows. God grant us grace on whatever path we take.

In the sandbox, Sophia yells happily as she decides what she wants to be when she grows up.

> SOPHIA
> Queen of England! That's what I'll be! Queen Sophia! Then I can live in a castle!

George removes his collar and hangs it on the coat rack.

> RANDALL
> Can we come to your inauguration?

> SOPHIA
> Of course! You're my special-est guests!

> MOTHER'S VOICE
> Sophie! Sophie!

> SOPHIA
> Oops. Time to go.

Sophia runs to the stool, passing George but not making eye contact. George moves to the sandbox, becoming six years old again.

Randall and Anne pretend not to notice him. They play the Prince and Princess of Wales with imaginary figures.

                    ANNE
     Prince Randall, Prince Randall, will
     you   marry   me   and   we'll   have
     seventeen children?

Silently, George slips into the sandbox, lonely and afraid.

                  RANDALL
     Later, Princess. I have to go kill
     dragons.

Randall clomps his imaginary horse away from the castle, making appropriate sound effects.

Sophia sits on the stool and puts on a sparkling tiara. Her banter with the audience is poised and warm. She gestures to the tiara.

                  SOPHIA
     The Queen of England, I'm not. But
     I've met her at a formal event.

She smiles happily.

SOPHIA (CONT'D)
My life has been charmed, even though I wasn't born into the royal family.

She laughs.

SOPHIA (CONT'D)
I'm Ambassador to France. Whoever would have thought? Before this appointment, I served sixteen years in the House of Representatives. Don't know how I got into politics. Just happened. Certainly wasn't the plan. In law school I started writing children's books. Somehow, they got published. Now there are sixteen. Can you believe it—sixteen! Movies made from two of them! Isn't it amazing! Between writing and politics, I've traveled all over the world. I speak seven languages. Not well, but I can order a hamburger on every continent.

She jumps off the stool and moves about the stage, a commanding, strong presence.

SOPHIA (CONT'D)

The world has spread itself out before me like a banquet table. I still ski. Still play in sandboxes. Bought a castle in Bordeaux. It's not much but it's still a castle. Randall and Anne came to visit last year. You remember them, don't you? My oldest and dearest friends. Of course, back then, they were Randy and Annie.

She gestures to the sandbox and shakes her head happily at the unexpected joys of life.

SOPHIA (CONT'D)
Yes, they DID get married. High school sweethearts. They live in Denver and have a paint shop. Doing very well. Three children. Annie had cancer five years ago but the treatments worked and she's in remission. Her strength never ceases to amaze me. Insurmountable odds and she pulls through. She grabs onto life and refuses to let go...Aw, Annie...so far away and still right here in my heart...

Sophia throws off her tiara and jumps into the sandbox as a delighted little girl, smiling happily at Anne. Anne looks up surprised and pleased.

ANNE
Hi!

Sophia spontaneously hugs Anne and Anne blinks.

SOPHIA
I love you, Annie! You are my bestest friend!

ANNE
I love you, too, Sophia! You're my bestest friend!

Anne pats Sophia sweetly on the head. Then Anne slips out of the sandbox and leans against it, aging years in the process. The children in the sandbox play silently.

Anne's face hardens. She is a mess, a junky. She reaches into her pocket and pulls out a strap, which she tightens around her arm.

ANNE (CONT'D)
Yeah.

With an imaginary needle, she injects heroin into a vein. Her eyes roll back in her head. Her head falls forward and then back, and her movements become slow and heavy.

ANNE (CONT'D)
Yeah, baby.

The hand holding the needle drops away from her arm. She fumbles with the strap and slowly frees it.

>   ANNE (CONT'D)
>   Give it.

Her eyes are dark and brooding as she goes into the nod. Her head drops twice and she opens her eyes and sees the audience. She stares at the audience with hatred and anger.

>   ANNE (CONT'D)
>   So?

Her eyes close and she fights to reopen them. She slurs, fighting to form the biting words.

>   ANNE (CONT'D)
>   So what? You think you're so much
>   better? Name of the game's sedation.
>   Right? Whole world's looking for a
>   way out.

She snorts and looks at the audience accusingly.

>   ANNE (CONT'D)
>   What's yours? Beer and TV?

She sarcastically taunts the audience.

>   ANNE (CONT'D)

You got the same look as Georgie Porgie. Remember Georgie? Little shit from the sandbox? Big Country and Western singer now. Waited for him behind the concert hall last night. Wanted to tell him he sang good.

She is vicious and angrily sarcastic.

ANNE (CONT'D)
Gave me a handout. Fifty bucks. Big spender. Fifty bucks. Didn't know me at first. Then he got that same look on his face. Same as you. "Aw, Annie," he said. "Aw, Annie."

She nods and snarls.

ANNE (CONT'D)
Go back to your Bud Lite. You know what you can do with that look.

She fades again as the drug washes through her. She opens her eyes but cannot focus on the audience anymore.

ANNE (CONT'D)
Big deal.

She nods again.

ANNE (CONT'D)
Big deal.

She nods out and lays still and unconscious, leaning against the sandbox.

In the sandbox, George yells angrily at Randall.

> GEORGE
> Yeah, and you'll go to jail too.

> RANDALL
> Who says?

> GEORGE
> I says.

> RANDALL
> I'm too smart. They can't catch me.

> GEORGE
> Nyah.

George throws imaginary sand at Randall.

> SOPHIA
> Georgie, stop that. Be nice.

Randall stands up as a little boy, brushing the sand off his pants. He moves toward the stool as he speaks, aging from a child to a stooped thug. He stands rocking on his heels, scrutinizing the audience with narrowed eyes, eyes that have seen really hard times. He speaks in a gruff, slang-laden voice.

> RANDALL
> I was wrong.

He nods and speaks slowly.

                    RANDALL (CONT'D)
Dey caught up wid me and I did eight
years. Thought I was so damn smart.
Speedin' through life. Smartest,
meanest, quickest dude that ever
lived. Just ask me. Dumb punk kid.
Let me tell ya somethin' about self-
destruction. It works. Ain't nobody can
pull ya out when ya don't let 'em.
Didn't learn nuttin' the first time. Had
to do it again. Thirteen years for
armed robbery.

Randall's tone remains sarcastic.

                    RANDALL (CONT'D)
Taught me to weld in prison. Me.
Welding. Joke, right?

Randall shakes his head and smiles.

                    RANDALL (CONT'D)
Got out two years ago. Started weldin'
for a living. Good money. Got a
girlfriend. Nice girl. Waitress. Started
lookin' at what I was weldin'. Started
messin' around with it. Sculpture.
Sculpture, man. No kiddin'.

He smiles broadly and chuckles.

                    RANDALL (CONT'D)
Goin' to art school now. And I like it.
Guess who I run into?

He looks up for an answer.

                    RANDALL (CONT'D)
Nah. You'll never guess. Sophie.
Sophie from the sandbox. Teaches
little kids how to draw.

He leans forward in confidence to the
audience.

                    RANDALL (CONT'D)
I think she's a lesbian. Don't matter, I
guess. Sophie's alright. Real quiet.
Real serious. Good with the kids.
She's alright.

Randall delights in the new world he has
made for himself since prison.

                    RANDALL (CONT'D)
They gave me a show. Real gallery
show. No way, you say. Some
collector even bought one. Gave it to
the city. Who woulda thought? It's in
the park. Maybe you seen it?
Somethin' to be proud of, alright. Real
proud. I done alright. Everything's real
good now.

He lifts his index finger to sign off and
saunters back toward the sandbox.

In the sandbox, George has teased Sophia
into a screaming fit.

                    SOPHIA
                 (shrieking)
Will too!

GEORGE
Will not!

Randall stops and pulls a toothpick from his pocket and sticks it in his mouth.

SOPHIA
Will too!

GEORGE
Will not!

Randall stands still, arms crossed, legs flexed, musing as he watches the fight between Sophia and George.

SOPHIA
I will too get married! And he'll be handsome and smart and funny and nice and not like you at all!

Sophia takes a swing at George, who ducks out of the way.

In a fury, Sophia jumps up and kicks George's toys.

GEORGE
Hey! My cars! My cars!

George wails in horror that Sophia has paid him back. Sophia jumps out of the sandbox and runs to the stool, sitting on the floor beside it.

George rubs his eyes and cries melodramatically.

                    GEORGE (CONT'D)
My cars. My cars.

He looks around to see if anyone is looking
and realizes he is all alone. Terror flashes
through his eyes. He pulls up his legs and
arms into a tight ball and looks around in
fear.

                    GEORGE (CONT'D)
My cars. My cars.

He begins to rock and slowly slips his
thumb into his mouth for comfort. He is a
frightened, lonely little boy.

Sophia glances at the audience through
downcast eyes. She keeps her head down.
She is nervous and exhausted. Her face is
old and haggard.

                    SOPHIA
When Frank started drinking heavy, I
shoulda left him. But I married him for
better or worse and I guess this is
worse. Ain't his fault, don't suppose.
He can't help it. Do my best to keep
him from hitting on the kids. At least
so the teachers don't see the marks.

Her eyes get distant.

                    SOPHIA (CONT'D)

Don't know. All seemed so easy when we was kids, playin' in the sandbox. Seemed like we coulda been anything. All we had to do was pick. Sometimes I wonder...

She hesitates and laughs nervously at herself. She gets up slowly, supporting herself with one hand on the stool on her unsteady legs.

SOPHIA (CONT'D)
Suppose this is gonna sound pretty dumb...But don't you ever wonder how maybe one thing—just one little thing—coulda made a whole lot of difference in your life? Like made it so different you wouldn't even reco'nize yourself? If I'd learned to draw, I coulda been an art teacher, livin' in my own apartment in some big city someplace. Or gone off to college. Coulda been a fancy lawyer, travellin' all over the world, talking fancy languages.

She sighs and brings herself back to reality.

SOPHIA (CONT'D)
Ain't so bad. Frank don't drink all the time. Ain't a bad man. Some days is pretty good. He bought me some Tupperware couple months ago so I know he still cares. Don't believe the stuff 'bout that bartender and him...

She's lying to herself and a tear trickles down her cheek, betraying her. She looks up at the audience, her eyes brimming.

> SOPHIA (CONT'D)
> Don't it make you wonder, though? How things maybe coulda been different? Like if I hadn't met Frank so young? Or if this or that had happened different?

She smiles faintly.

> SOPHIA (CONT'D)
> When we was kids in the sandbox, I wanted to be Queen of England.

She shrugs.

> SOPHIA (CONT'D)
> Maybe I coulda been. Maybe there's a life out there for me I don't even know about. Maybe a whole bunch of lives I coulda had. It's like when we was playin' in the sandbox, there was a bunch of roads all leadin' in different directions. And we just picked one and headed out for wherever it was gonna take us. Takin' this trail or that along the way. And the scenery just kept changin', ya know? Pretty amazin' trip. And we kept making decisions about this road or that one, and all those decisions, all those choices, they took us someplace.

She walks over to Randall. They look at each other.

                    SOPHIA (CONT'D)
          All them trails in the forest. Look
          where it lead you.

                    RANDALL
          Every choice I made took me down a
          different path. So many possibilities,
          so many trails through the forest.

Sophia and Randall join hands and walk to the sandbox, looking at Georgie, who looks up at them with fear in his eyes.

                    GEORGE
          I was so scared.

                    RANDALL
          We're all scared.

                    SOPHIA
          But it's like opening Christmas
          presents and seeing what's inside,
          like Annie said.

Randall and Sophia reach out their hands to George. George takes their hands and they help him up.

The three approach Anne, who is still on the nod, leaning against the sandbox. Sophia kneels down beside her.

                    SOPHIA (CONT'D)

Annie? Annie?

Anne slowly opens her eyes and looks at Sophia. She manages a weak smile.

> SOPHIA (CONT'D)
> You can get up now, Annie. Everything's going to be all right.

> ANNE
> It is?

> SOPHIA
> Randy and Georgie are here to help too.

> RANDALL
> Hello, Annie.

> GEORGE
> Hi, pretty girl.

Anne looks at the three of them, from one to the other.

> GEORGE (CONT'D)
> I know your castle is broken.

> RANDALL
> We can build it again, Annie. Even better.

Anne starts to cry. Sophia pats her on the shoulder.

> SOPHIA
> Don't cry, Annie.

GEORGE
You can hold onto me.

SOPHIA
Grab onto us, Annie. Grab onto life and don't let go.

Anne reaches for Randall and George who help her up, as does Sophia. The four of them look at each other and the tears and sadness slowly give way to sheepish grins. The giggles start and soon all four are laughing. Randall stomps his feet and Sophia hugs Anne.

George jumps into the sandbox.

GEORGE
Vroom. Vroom. Bee-beep!

Randall imitates flying a jet through the air. Sophia and Anne, their arms around each other, watch the hijinks and tighten their hug.

THE END

Burro Race

About the Author:

Carol Bellhouse is an attorney, writer and photographer living in Leadville, Colorado. At 10,100 feet, life has never been boring. She travels to great places like New Zealand, Hawaii and the catacombs underlying Paris.

An award-winning playwright and screenwriter, *Fire Drifter 2: Meteor Shower* is the second novel in the series. She has previously published two poetry books, *Loving the Cowboy* and *Never More Beautiful*, and a biography, *Vegas Dynasty: The Story of Darwin Lamb.*

Current projects include another book of poetry, a young adult series titled *Mining Stardust,* and Madelyn Tremaine's continuing adventures in *Fire Drifter*.

Website: www.CarolBellhouse.com

Twin Lakes

Scripts by Carol Bellhouse:

Meteor Shower
Edge
Guido, My Guardian Angel
Cross Roads
Crystal Carnival
Kill for You
Anorexic Psycho Killers of Leadville
Ice
Ghosts in the Graveyard
The Vessel
Dancing in the Sand
Stacy
Missing Pieces
Strawberries, Brooms and Pelicans
Unfinished Conversation
Marilyn
Vegas Knights

Leadville

Acknowledgements:

Many thanks to my daughter Whitney and son Mike for soldiering on as the Zen Masters in my life; Dawn Beck for holding up my weight through the process and divining everything techie; Laurel McHargue for being fun and excited; Roger Johnson, Sharon Furman Bland, and the Monday Writers Group for supplying buckets of confidence; Allison Finney Maruska and Jenny Po Loyd for being my Plausibility Police; Curtis Imrie for being my film-industry expert; Erin Grantham for great feedback; and Tina Erickson Westphal for typing, typing, typing and reading my mind about what goes where.

Made in the USA
San Bernardino, CA
23 November 2013